A STONE CREEK CHRISTMAS

LINDA LAEL MILLER

THORNDIKE
CHIVERS

This Large Print edition is published by Thorndike Press, Waterville, Maine, USA and by AudioGo Ltd, Bath, England.
Thorndike Press, a part of Gale, Cengage Learning.
Copyright © 2008 by Linda Lael Miller.
The moral right of the author has been asserted.

LIBRARY OF CONGRESS CATALOGING-IN-PUBLICATION DATA

Miller, Linda Lael.
   A Stone Creek Christmas / by Linda Lael Miller.
     p. cm. — (Thorndike Press large print famous authors)
   ISBN-13: 978-1-4104-2429-7
   ISBN-10: 1-4104-2429-4
   1. Large type books. 2. Christmas stories. 3. Single fathers.
I. Title.
PS3563.I41373S76 2010
813'.54—dc22   2010021760

BRITISH LIBRARY CATALOGUING-IN-PUBLICATION DATA AVAILABLE
Published in 2010 in the U.S. by arrangement with Harlequin Books S.A.
Published in 2011 in the U.K. by arrangement with Harlequin Enterprises II B.V.

U.K. Hardcover: 978 1 408 49307 6 (Chivers Large Print)
U.K. Softcover: 978 1 408 49308 3 (Camden Large Print)

Printed and bound in Great Britain by the MPG Books Group

1 2 3 4 5 6 7 14 13 12 11 10

For Sandi Howlett, dog foster mom,
with love.
Thank you.

CHAPTER ONE

Sometimes, especially in the dark of night, when pure exhaustion sank Olivia O'Ballivan, DVM, into deep and stuporous sleep, she heard them calling — the finned, the feathered, the four-legged.

Horses, wild or tame, dogs beloved and dogs lost, far from home, cats abandoned alongside country roads because they'd become a problem for someone, or left behind when an elderly owner died.

The neglected, the abused, the unwanted, the lonely.

Invariably, the message was the same: *Help me.*

Even when Olivia tried to ignore the pleas, telling herself she was only *dreaming,* she invariably sprang to full wakefulness as though she'd been catapulted from the bottom of a canyon. It didn't matter how many eighteen-hour days she'd worked, between making stops at farms and ranches all over the county, putting in her time at the veterinary clinic in Stone Creek, overseeing the plans for the new, state-of-the-art shelter her famous big brother, Brad, a country musician, was building with the proceeds from a movie he'd starred in.

Tonight it was a reindeer.

Olivia sat blinking in her tousled bed, trying to catch her breath. Shoved both hands through her short dark hair. Her current foster dog, Ginger, woke up, too, stretching, yawning.

A reindeer?

"O'Ballivan," she told herself, flinging off the covers to sit up on the edge of the mattress, "you've really gone around the bend this time."

But the silent cry persisted, plaintive and confused.

Olivia only sometimes heard actual words when the animals spoke, though Ginger was articulate — generally, it was more of an unformed concept made up of strong emotion and often images, somehow coalescing into an intuitive imperative. But she could see the reindeer clearly in her mind's eye, standing on a frozen roadway, bewildered.

She recognized the adjoining driveway as her own. A long way down, next to the tilted mailbox on the main road. The poor creature wasn't hurt — just lost. Hungry and thirsty, too — and terribly afraid. Easy prey for hungry wolves and coyotes.

"There are no reindeer in Arizona," Olivia told Ginger, who looked skeptical as she hauled her arthritic yellow Lab/golden retriever self up off her comfy bed in the corner of Olivia's cluttered bedroom. "Absolutely, positively, no doubt about it, there *are no reindeer in Arizona.*"

"Whatever," Ginger replied with another yawn, already heading for the door as Olivia pulled sweatpants on over her boxer pajama bottoms. She tugged a hoodie, left over from one of her brother's preretirement concert tours, over her head and jammed her feet into the totally unglamorous work boots she wore to wade through pastures and barns.

Olivia lived in a small rental house in the country, though once the shelter was finished, she'd be moving into a spacious apartment upstairs, living in town. She drove an old gray Suburban that had belonged to her late grandfather, called Big John by everyone who knew him, and did not aspire to anything fancier. She had not exactly been feathering her nest since she'd graduated from veterinary school.

Her twin sisters, Ashley and Melissa, were constantly after her to 'get her act together,' find herself a man, have a family. Both of them were single, with no glimmer of honeymoon cottages and white picket fences on the horizon, so in Olivia's opinion, they didn't have a lot of room to talk. It was just that she was a few years older than they were, that was all.

Anyway, it wasn't as if she didn't want those things — she did — but between her practice and the "Dr. Dolittle routine," as Brad referred to her admittedly weird animal-communication skills, there simply weren't enough hours in the day to do it all.

Since the rental house was old, the garage was detached. Olivia and Ginger made their way through a deep, powdery field of snow. The Suburban was no spiffy rig — most of the time it was splattered with muddy slush and worse — but it always ran, in any kind of weather. And it would go practically any-where.

"Try getting to a stranded reindeer in that sporty little red number Melissa drives," Olivia told Ginger as she shoved up the garage door. "Or that silly hybrid of Ash-ley's."

"I wouldn't mind taking a spin in the sports car," Ginger replied, plodding gamely up the special wooden steps Olivia dragged over to the passenger side of the Suburban.

Ginger was getting older, after all, and her joints gave her problems, especially since her "accident." Certain concessions had to be made.

"Fat chance," Olivia said, pushing back the steps once Ginger was settled in the shotgun seat, then closing the car door. Moments later she was sliding in on the driver's side, shoving the key into the ignition, cranking up the geriatric engine. "You know how Melissa is about dog hair. You might tear a hole in her fancy leather upholstery with one of those Fu-Manchu toenails of yours."

"She likes dogs," Ginger insisted with a magnanimous lift of her head. *"It's just that she thinks she's allergic."* Ginger always believed the best of everyone in particular and humanity in general, even though she'd been ditched alongside a highway, with two of her legs fractured, after her first owner's vengeful boyfriend had tossed her out of a moving car. Olivia had come along a few minutes later, homing in on the mystical distress call bouncing between her head and her heart, and rushed Ginger to the clinic, where she'd had multiple surgeries and a long, difficult recovery.

Olivia flipped on the windshield wipers, but she still squinted to see through the huge, swirling flakes. "My sister," she said, "is a hypochondriac."

"It's just that Melissa hasn't met the right dog yet," Ginger maintained. *"Or the right man."*

"Don't start about men," Olivia retorted, peering out, looking for the reindeer.

"He's out there, you know," Ginger remarked, panting as she gazed out at the snowy night.

"The reindeer or the man?"

"Both," Ginger said with a dog smile.

"What am I going to do with a reindeer?"

"You'll think of something," Ginger replied. *"It's almost Christmas. Maybe there's an APB from the North Pole. I'd check Santa's Web site if I had opposable thumbs."*

"Funny," Olivia said, not the least bit amused. "If you had opposable thumbs, you'd order things off infomercials just because you like the UPS man so much. We'd be inundated with get-rich-quick real estate courses, herbal weight loss programs and stuff to whiten our teeth." The ever-present ache between her shoulder blades knotted itself up tighter as she scanned the darkness on either side of the narrow driveway. Christmas. One more thing she didn't have the time for, let alone the requisite enthusiasm, but Brad and his new wife,

Meg, would put up a big tree right after Thanksgiving, hunt her down and shanghai her if she didn't show up for the family festival at Stone Creek Ranch, especially since Mac had come along six months before, and this was Baby's First Christmas. And because Carly, Meg's teenage sister, was spending the semester in Italy, as part of a special program for gifted students, and both Brad and Meg missed her to distraction. Ashley would throw her annual open house at the bed-and-breakfast, and Melissa would probably decide she was allergic to mistletoe and holly and develop convincing symptoms.

Olivia would go, of course. To Brad and Meg's because she loved them, and *adored* Mac. To Ashley's open house because she loved her kid sister, too, and could mostly forgive her for being Martha Stewart incarnate. Damn, she'd even pick up nasal spray and chicken soup for Melissa, though she drew the line at actually cooking.

"There's Blitzen," Ginger said, adding a cheerful yip.

Sure enough, the reindeer loomed in the snow-speckled cones of gold from the headlights.

Olivia put on the brakes, shifted the engine into neutral. "You stay here," she said, pushing open the door.

"Like I'm going outside in this *weather,"* Ginger said with a sniff.

Slowly Olivia approached the reindeer. The creature was small, definitely a miniature breed, with eyes big and dark and luminous in the light from the truck, and it stood motionless.

"Lost," it told her, not having Ginger's extensive vocabulary. If she ever found a loving home for that dog, she'd miss the long conversations, even though they had very different political views.

The deer had antlers, which meant it was male.

"Hey, buddy," she said. "Where did you come from?"

"Lost," the reindeer repeated. Either he was dazed or not particularly bright. Like humans, animals were unique beings, some of them Einsteins, most of them ordinary joes.

"Are you hurt?" she asked, to be certain. Her intuition was rarely wrong where such things were concerned, but there was always the off chance.

Nothing.

She approached, slowly and carefully. Ran skillful hands over pertinent parts of the animal. No blood, no obvious breaks, though sprains and hairline fractures were a possibility. No identifying tags or notched ears.

The reindeer stood still for the examination, which might have meant he was tame, though Olivia couldn't be certain of that. Nearly every animal she encountered, wild or otherwise, allowed her within touching distance. Once, with help from Brad and Jesse McKettrick, she'd treated a wounded stallion who'd never been shod, fitted with a halter, or ridden.

"You're gonna be okay now," she told the little deer. It *did* look as though it ought to be hitched to Santa's sleigh. There was a silvery cast to its coat, its antlers were delicately etched and it was petite — barely bigger than Ginger.

She cocked a thumb toward the truck. "Can you follow me to my place, or shall I put you in the back?" she asked.

The reindeer ducked its head. Shy, then. And weary.

"But you've already traveled a long way, haven't you?" Olivia went on.

She opened the back of the Suburban, pulled out the sturdy ramp she always carried for Ginger and other four-legged passengers no longer nimble enough to make the jump.

The deer hesitated, probably catching

15

Ginger's scent.

"Not to worry," Olivia said. "Ginger's a lamb. Hop aboard there, Blitzen."

"His name is Rodney," Ginger announced. She'd turned, forefeet on the console, to watch them over the backseat.

"On Dasher, on Dancer, on Prancer or — Rodney," Olivia said, gesturing, but giving the animal plenty of room.

Rodney raised his head at the sound of his name, seemed to perk up a little. Then he pranced right up the ramp, into the back of the Suburban, and lay down on a bed of old feed sacks with a heavy reindeer snort.

Olivia closed the back doors of the rig as quietly as she could, so Rodney wouldn't be startled.

"How did you know his name?" Olivia asked once she was back in the driver's seat. "All I'm getting from him is 'Lost.' "

"He told me," Ginger said. *"He's not ready to go into a lot of detail about his past. There's a touch of amnesia, too. Brought on by the emotional trauma of losing his way."*

"Have you been watching soap operas again, while I'm away working? *Dr. Phil? Oprah?*"

"Only when you forget and leave the TV on when you go out. I don't have opposable thumbs, remember?"

16

Olivia shoved the recalcitrant transmission into reverse, backed into a natural turn-around and headed back up the driveway toward the house. She supposed she should have taken Rodney to the clinic for X-rays, or over to the homeplace, where there was a barn, but it was the middle of the night, after all.

If she went to the clinic, all the boarders would wake up, barking and meowing fit to wake the whole town. If she went to Stone Creek Ranch, she'd probably wake the baby, and both Brad and Meg were sleep deprived as it was.

So Rodney would have to spend what remained of the night on the enclosed porch. She'd make him a bed with some of the old blankets she kept on hand, give him water, see if he wouldn't nosh on a few of Ginger's kibbles. In the morning she'd attend to him properly. Take him to town for those X-rays and a few blood tests, haul him to Brad's if he was well enough to travel, fix him up with a stall of his own. Get him some deer chow from the feed and grain.

Rodney drank a whole bowl of water once Olivia had coaxed him up the steps and through the outer door onto the enclosed porch. He kept a watchful eye on Ginger, though she didn't growl or make any sud-

17

den moves, the way some dogs would have done.

Instead, Ginger gazed up at Olivia, her soulful eyes glowing with practical compassion. *"I'd better sleep out here with Rodney,"* she said. *"He's still pretty scared. The washing machine has him a little spooked."*

This was a great concession on Ginger's part, for she loved her wide, fluffy bed. Ashley had made it for her, out of the softest fleece she could find, and even monogrammed the thing. Olivia smiled at the image of her blond, curvaceous sister seated at her beloved sewing machine, whirring away.

"You're a good dog," she said, her eyes burning a little as she bent to pat Ginger's head.

Ginger sighed. Another day, another noble sacrifice, the sound seemed to say.

Olivia went into her bedroom and got Ginger's bed. Put it on the floor for her. Carried the water bowl back to the kitchen for a refill.

When she returned to the porch the second time, Rodney was lying on the cherished dog bed, and Ginger was on the pile of old blankets.

"Ginger, your bed — ?"

Ginger yawned yet again, rested her muzzle on her forelegs and rolled her eyes

18

upward. *"Everybody needs a soft place to land,"* she said sleepily. *"Even reindeer."*

The pony was not a happy camper.

Tanner Quinn leaned against the stall door. He'd just bought Starcross Ranch, and Butterpie, his daughter's pet, had arrived that day, trucked in by a horse-delivery outfit hired by his sister, Tessa, along with his own palomino gelding, Shiloh.

Shiloh was settling in just fine. Butterpie was having a harder time of it.

Tanner sighed, shifted his hat to the back of his head. He probably should have left Shiloh and Butterpie at his sister's place in Kentucky, where they'd had all that fabled bluegrass to run in and munch on, since the ranch wasn't going to be his permanent home, or theirs. He'd picked it up as an investment, at a fire-sale price, and would live there while he oversaw the new construction project in Stone Creek — a year at the outside.

It was the latest in a long line of houses that never had time to become homes. He came to each new place, bought a house or a condo, built something big and sleek and expensive, then moved on, leaving the property he'd temporarily occupied in the hands of some eager real estate agent.

The new project, an animal shelter, was not his usual thing — he normally designed and erected office buildings, multimillion-dollar housing compounds for movie stars and moguls, and the occasional government-sponsored school, bridge or hospital, somewhere on foreign soil — usually hostile. Before his wife, Katherine, died five years ago, she'd traveled with him, bringing Sophie along.

But then —

Tanner shook off the memory. Thinking about the way Katherine had been killed required serious bourbon, and he'd been off the sauce for a long time. He'd never developed a drinking problem, but the warning signs had been there, and he'd decided to save Sophie — and himself — the extra grief. He'd put the cork back in the bottle and left it there for good.

It should have been him, not Kat. That was as far as he could go, sober.

He shifted his attention back to the little cream-colored pony standing forlornly in its fancy new stall. He was no vet, but he didn't have to be to diagnose the problem. The horse missed Sophie, now ensconced in a special high-security boarding school in Connecticut.

He missed her, too. More than the horse did, for sure. But she was *safe* in that high-walled and distant place — safe from the factions who'd issued periodic death threats over things he'd built. The school was like a fortress — he'd designed it himself, and his best friend, Jack McCall, a Special Forces veteran and big-time security consultant, had installed the systems. They were top-of-the-line, best available. The children and grandchildren of presidents, congressmen, Oscar winners and software inventors attended that school — it had to be kidnap-proof, and it was.

Sophie had begged him not to leave her there.

Even as Tanner reflected on that, his cell phone rang. Sophie had chosen the ring tone before their most recent parting — the theme song from *How the Grinch Stole Christmas.*

He, of course, was the Grinch.

"Tanner Quinn," he said, even though he knew this wasn't a business call. The habit was ingrained.

"I *hate* this place!" Sophie blurted without preamble. "It's like a *prison!*"

"Soph," Tanner began, on another sigh. "Your roommate sings lead for your favorite rock band of all time. How bad can it be?"

"I want to come home!"

If only we had one, Tanner thought. The barely palatable reality was that he and Sophie had lived like Gypsies — if not actual fugitives — since Kat's death.

"Honey, you know I won't be here long. You'd make friends, get settled in and then it would be time to move on again."

"I want you," Sophie all but wailed. Tanner's heart caught on a beat. "I want Butterpie. I want to be a *regular kid!*"

Sophie would never be a "regular kid." She was only twelve and already taking college-level courses — another advantage of attending an elite school. The classes were small, the computers were powerful enough to guide satellites and the visiting lecturers were world-renowned scientists, historians, linguistics experts and mathematical superstars.

"Honey —"

"Why can't I live in Stoner Creek, with you and Butterpie?"

A smile tugged at one corner of Tanner's mouth. "*Stone* Creek," he said. "If there are any stoners around here, I haven't made their acquaintance yet."

Not that he'd really made *anybody's* acquaintance. He hadn't been in town more than a few days. He knew the real estate agent who'd sold him Starcross, and Brad O'Ballivan, because he'd built a palace for him once, outside Nashville, which was how he'd gotten talked into the animal-shelter contract.

Brad O'Ballivan. He'd thought the hot-shot country-and-western music star would never settle down. Now he was over-the-top in love with his bride, Meg, and wanted all his friends married off, too. He probably figured if he could fall that hard for a woman out here in Noplace, U.S.A., Tanner might, too.

"Dad, please," Sophie said, sniffling now. Somehow his daughter's brave attempt to suck it up got to Tanner even more than the crying had. "Get me out of here. If I can't come to Stone Creek, maybe I could stay with Aunt Tessa again, like I did last summer. . . ."

Tanner took off his hat, moved along the breezeway to the barn doorway, shut off the lights. "You know your aunt is going through a rough time right now," he said quietly. *A rough time?* Tessa and her no-account husband, Paul Barker, were getting a divorce. Among other things, Barker had gotten another woman pregnant — a real blow to Tess, who'd wanted a child ever since she'd hit puberty — and now she was fighting to

23

hold on to her home. She'd bought that horse farm with her own money, having been a successful TV actress in her teens, and poured everything she had into it — including the contents of her investment portfolio. Against Tanner's advice, she hadn't insisted on a prenup.

We're in love, she'd told him, starry-eyed with happiness.

Paul Barker hadn't had the proverbial pot to piss in, of course. And within a month of the wedding he'd been a signer on every account Tess had. As the marriage deteriorated, so did Tess's wealth.

Cold rage jangled along Tanner's nerves, followed the fault line in his soul. At Kat's suggestion, he'd set up a special trust fund for Tess, way back, and it was a damn good thing he had. To this day, she didn't know the money existed — he and Kat hadn't wanted Barker to tap in to it — and when she did find out, her fierce Quinn pride would probably force her to refuse it.

At least if she lost the horse farm to Barker and his dream team of lawyers — more like *nightmare* team — she'd have the means to start over. The question was, would she have the *heart* to make a new beginning?

"Dad?" Sophie asked. "Are you still there?"

"I'm here," Tanner said, looking around at the night-shrouded landscape surrounding him. There must have been a foot of snow on the ground already, with more coming down. Hell, November wasn't even over yet.

"Couldn't I at least come home for Christmas?"

"Soph, we don't *have* a home, remember?"

She was sniffling again. "Sure we do," she said very softly. "Home is where you and Butterpie are."

Tanner's eyes stung all of a sudden. He told himself it was the bitterly cold weather. When he'd finally agreed to take the job, he'd thought, *Arizona.* Cacti. Sweeping desert vistas. Eighty-degree winters.

But Stone Creek was in *northern* Arizona, near Flagstaff, a place of timber and red rock — and the occasional blizzard.

It wasn't like him to overlook that kind of geographical detail, but he had. He'd signed on the dotted line because the money was good and because Brad was a good friend.

"How about if I come back there? We'll spend Christmas in New York — skate at Rockefeller Center, see the Rockettes —"

Sophie loved New York. She planned to

attend college there, and then medical school, and eventually set up a practice as a neurosurgeon. No small-time goals for *his* kid, but then, the doctor gene had come from Kat, not him. Kat. As beautiful as a model and as smart as they come, she'd been a surgeon, specializing in pediatric cardiology. She'd given all that up, swearing it was only temporary, to have Sophie. To travel the world with her footloose husband . . .

"But then I wouldn't get to see Butterpie," Sophie protested. A raw giggle escaped her. "I don't think they'd let her stay at the Waldorf with us, even if we paid a pet deposit."

Tanner pictured the pony nibbling on the ubiquitous mongo flower arrangement in the hotel's sedate lobby, with its Cole Porter piano, dropping a few road apples on the venerable old carpets. And he grinned. "Probably not."

"Don't you want me with you, Dad?" Sophie spoke in a small voice. "Is that it? My friend Cleta says her mom won't let her come home for Christmas because she's got a new boyfriend and she doesn't want a kid throwing a wet blanket on the action."

Cleta. Who named a poor, defenseless kid Cleta?

And what kind of person put "action" before their own child, especially at Christmas?

Tanner closed his eyes, walking toward the dark house he didn't know his way around in yet, since he'd spent the first couple of nights at Brad's, waiting for the power to be turned on and the phones hooked up. Guilt stabbed through his middle. "I love you more than anything or anybody else in the world," he said gruffly, and he meant it. Practically everything he did was geared to provide for Sophie, to protect her from the nameless, faceless forces who hated him. "Trust me, there's no *action* going on around here."

"I'm going to run away, then," she said resolutely.

"Good luck," Tanner replied after sucking in a deep breath. "That school is hermetically sealed, kiddo. You know that as well as I do."

"What are you so afraid of?"

Losing you. The kid had no way of knowing how big, and how dangerous, the world was. She'd been just seven years old when Kat was killed, and barely remembered the long flight home from northern Africa, private bodyguards occupying the seats

27

around them, the sealed coffin, the media blitz.

"U.S. Contractor Targeted by Insurgent Group," one headline had read. "Wife of American Businessman Killed in Possible Revenge Shooting."

"I'm not afraid of anything," Tanner lied.

"It's because of what happened to Mom," Sophie insisted. "That's what Aunt Tessa says."

"Aunt Tessa ought to mind her own business."

"If you don't come and get me, I'm breaking out of here. And there's no telling where I'll go."

Tanner had reached the old-fashioned wraparound porch. The place had a certain charm, though it needed a lot of fixing up. He could picture Sophie there all too easily, running back and forth to the barn, riding a yellow bus to school, wearing jeans instead of uniforms. Tacking up posters on her bedroom walls and holding sleepovers with ordinary friends instead of junior celebrities and other mini-jet-setters.

"Don't try it, Soph," he said, fumbling with the knob, shouldering open the heavy front door. "You're fine at Briarwood, and it's a long way between Connecticut and Arizona."

"Fine?" Sophie shot back. "This place isn't in a parallel dimension, you know. Things *happen.* Marissa Worth got ptomaine from the potato salad in the cafeteria, just last week, and had to be airlifted to Walter Reed. Allison Mooreland's appendix ruptured, and —"

"Soph," Tanner said, flipping on the lights in the entryway.

Which way was the kitchen?

His room was upstairs someplace, but where?

He hung up his hat, shrugged off his leather coat, tossed it in the direction of an ornate brass peg designed for the purpose.

Sophie didn't say a word. All the way across country, Tanner could feel her holding her breath.

"How's this? School lets out in May. You can come out here then. Spend the summer. Ride Butterpie all you want."

"I might be too big to ride her by summer," Sophie pointed out. Tanner wondered, as he often did, if his daughter wouldn't make a better lawyer than a doctor. "Thanksgiving is in three days," she went on in a rush. "Let me come home for that, and if you still don't think I'm a good kid to have around, I'll come back to Briarwood for the rest of the year and pretend I love it."

"It's not that I don't think you're a good kid, Soph." In the living room by then, Tanner paused to consult a yellowed wall calendar left behind by the ranch's previous owner. Unfortunately, it was several years out of date.

Sophie didn't answer.

"Thanksgiving is in three days?" Tanner muttered, dismayed. Living the way he did, he tended to lose track of holidays, but it figured that if Christmas was already a factor, turkey day had to be bearing down hard.

"I could still get a ticket if I flew standby," Sophie said hopefully.

Tanner closed his eyes. Let his forehead rest against the wall where a million little tack holes testified to all the calendars that had gone before this one. "That's a long way to travel for a turkey special in some greasy spoon," he said quietly. He knew the kid was probably picturing a Norman Rockwell scenario — old woman proudly presenting a golden-brown gobbler to a beaming family crowded around a table.

"Someone will invite you to Thanksgiving dinner," Sophie said, with a tone of bright, brittle bravery in her voice, "and I could just tag along."

He checked his watch, started for the kitchen. If it wasn't where he thought it was, he'd have to search until he found it, because he needed coffee. Hold the Jack Daniel's.

"You've been watching the Hallmark Channel again," he said wearily, his heart trying to scramble up his windpipe into the back of his throat. There were so many things he couldn't give Sophie — a stable home, a family, an ordinary childhood. But he *could* keep her safe, and that meant staying at Briarwood.

A long, painful pause ensued.

"You're not going to give in, are you?" Sophie asked finally, practically in a whisper.

"Are you just figuring that out, shortstop?" Tanner retorted, trying for a light tone.

She huffed out a weight-of-the-world sigh. "Okay, then," she replied, "don't say I didn't warn you."

CHAPTER TWO

It was a pity Starcross Ranch had fallen into such a state of disrepair, Olivia thought as she steered the Suburban down the driveway to the main road, Ginger beside her in the passenger seat, Rodney in the back. The place bordered her rental to the west, and although she passed the sagging rail fences and the tilting barn every day on her way to town, that morning the sight seemed even lonelier than usual.

She braked for the stop sign, looked both ways. No cars coming, but she didn't pull out right away. The vibe hit her before she could shift out of neutral and hit the gas.

"Oh, no," she said aloud.

Ginger, busy surveying the snowy countryside, offered no comment.

"Did you hear that?" Olivia persisted.

Ginger turned to look at her. Gave a little yip. Today, evidently, she was pretending to be an ordinary dog — as if *any* dog was ordinary — incapable of intelligent conversation.

The call was coming from the ancient barn on the Starcross property.

Olivia took a moment to rest her forehead on the cold steering wheel. She'd known Brad's friend the big-time contractor was moving in, of course, and she'd seen at least one moving truck, but she hadn't known there were any animals involved.

"I could ignore this," she said to Ginger.

"Or not," Ginger answered.

"Oh, hell," Olivia said. Then she signaled for a left turn — Stone Creek was in the other direction — and headed for the decrepit old gate marking the entrance to Starcross Ranch.

The gate stood wide open. No sheep or cattle then, probably, Olivia reasoned. Even greenhorns knew livestock tended to stray at every opportunity. Still, *some* kind of critter was sending out a psychic SOS from that pitiful barn.

They bumped up the rutted driveway, fishtailing a little on the slick snow and the layer of ice underneath, and Olivia tooted her horn. A spiffy new red pickup stood in front of the house, looking way too fancy for the neighborhood, but nobody appeared to see who was honking.

Muttering, Olivia brought the Suburban to a rattling stop in front of the barn, got out and shut the door hard.

"Hello?" she called.

No answer. Not from a human being, anyway.

The animal inside the barn amped up the psychic summons.

Olivia sprinted toward the barn door, glancing upward once at the sagging roof as she entered, with some trepidation. The place ought to be condemned. "Hello?" she repeated.

It took a moment for her eyes to adjust to the dimmer light, since the weather was dazzle-bright, though cold enough to crystallize her bone marrow.

"Over here," said a silent voice, deep and distinctly male.

Olivia ventured deeper into the shadows. The ruins of a dozen once-sturdy stalls lined the sawdust-and-straw aisle. She found two at the very back, showing fresh-lumber signs of recent restoration efforts.

A tall palomino regarded her from the stall on the right, tossed his head as if to indicate the one opposite.

Olivia went to that stall and looked over the half gate to see a small, yellowish-white pony gazing up at her in befuddled sorrow.

34

The horse lay forlornly in fresh wood shavings, its legs folded underneath.

Although she was technically trespassing, Olivia couldn't resist unlatching the gate and slipping inside. She crouched beside the pony, stroked its nose, patted its neck, gave its forelock an affectionate tug.

"Hey, there," she said softly. "What's all the fuss about?"

A slight shudder went through the little horse.

"She misses Sophie," the palomino said, from across the aisle.

Wondering who Sophie was, Olivia examined the pony while continuing to pet her. The animal was sound, well fed and well cared for in general.

The palomino nickered loudly, and that should have been a cue, but Olivia was too focused on the pony to pay attention.

"Who are you and what the hell are you doing sneaking around in my barn?" demanded a low, no-nonsense voice.

Olivia whirled, and toppled backward into the straw. Looked up to see a dark-haired man glowering down at her from over the stall gate. His eyes matched his blue denim jacket, and his Western hat looked a little too new.

"Who's Sophie?" she asked, getting to her

feet, dusting bits of straw off her jeans.

He merely folded his arms and glared. He'd asked the first question and, apparently, he intended to have the first answer. From the set of his broad shoulders, she guessed he'd wait for it until hell froze over if necessary.

Olivia relented, since she had rounds to make and a reindeer owner to track down. She summoned up her best smile and stuck out her hand. "Olivia O'Ballivan," she said. "I'm your neighbor — sort of — and . . ." *And I heard your pony calling out for help?* No, she couldn't say that. It was all too easy to imagine the reaction she'd get. "And since I'm a veterinarian, I always like to stop by when somebody new moves in. Offer my services."

The blue eyes sized her up, clearly found her less than statuesque. "You must deal mostly with cats and poodles," he said. "As you can see, I have horses."

Olivia felt the sexist remark like the unexpected back-snap of a rubber band, stinging and sudden. Adrenaline coursed through her, and she had to wait a few moments for it to subside. "This horse," she said when she'd regained her dignity, indicating the pony with a gesture of one hand, "is depressed."

One dark eyebrow quirked upward, and the hint of a smile played at the corner of Tanner Quinn's supple-looking mouth. That had to be who he was, since he'd said "*I have horses,*" not "we" or "they." Anyhow, he didn't look like an ordinary ranch hand.

"Does she need to take happy pills?" he asked.

"She wants Sophie," the palomino said, though of course Mr. Quinn didn't hear.

"Who's Sophie?" Olivia repeated calmly.

Quinn hesitated for a long moment. "My daughter," he finally said. "How do you happen to know her name?"

Olivia thought fast. "My brother must have mentioned her," she answered, heading for the stall door and hoping he'd step back so she could pass.

He didn't. Instead, he stood there like a support beam, his forearms resting on top of the door. "O'Ballivan," he mused. "You're Brad's sister? The one who'll be running the shelter when it's finished?"

"I think I just said Brad is my brother," Olivia replied, somewhat tartly. She felt strangely shaken and a little cornered, which was odd, because she wasn't claustrophobic and despite her unremarkable height of five feet three inches, she knew how to defend herself. "Now, would you mind letting me out of this stall?"

Quinn stepped back, even executed a sweeping bow.

"You're not leaving, are you?" the palomino fretted. *"Butterpie needs help."*

"Give me a second here," Olivia told the concerned horse. "I'll make sure Butterpie is taken care of, but it's going to take time." An awkward moment passed before she realized she'd spoken out loud, instead of using mental e-mail.

Quinn blocked her way again, planting himself in the middle of the barn aisle, and refolded his arms. "Now," he said ominously, "I *know* I've never mentioned that pony's name to anybody in Stone Creek, including Brad."

Olivia swallowed, tried for a smile but slid right down the side of it without catching hold. "Lucky guess," she said, and started around him.

He caught hold of her arm to stop her, but let go immediately.

Olivia stared up at him. The palomino was right; she couldn't leave, no matter how foolish she might seem to Tanner Quinn. Butterpie was in trouble.

"Who are you?" Tanner insisted gruffly.

"I told you. I'm Olivia O'Ballivan."

Tanner took off his hat with one hand,

38

shoved the other through his thick, some-what shaggy hair. The light was better in the aisle, since there were big cracks in the roof to let in the silvery sunshine, and she saw that he needed a shave.

He gave a heavy sigh. "Could we start over, here?" he asked. "If you're who you say you are, then we're going to be working together on the shelter project. That'll be a whole lot easier if we get along."

"Butterpie misses your daughter," Olivia said. "*Severely.* Where is she?"

Tanner sighed again. "Boarding school," he answered, as though the words had been pried out of him. The denim-colored eyes were still fixed on her face.

"Oh," Olivia answered, feeling sorry for the pony *and* Sophie. "She'll be home for Thanksgiving, though, right? Your daughter, I mean?"

Tanner's jawline looked rigid, and his eyes didn't soften. "No," he said.

"No?" Olivia's spirits, already on the dip, deflated completely.

He stepped aside. Before, he'd blocked her way. Now he obviously wanted her gone, ASAP.

It was Olivia's turn with the folded arms and stubborn stance. "Then I have to explain that to the horse," she said.

Tanner blinked. "What?"

She turned, went back to Butterpie's stall, opened the door and stepped inside. *"Sophie's away at boarding school,"* she told the animal silently. *"And she can't make it home for Thanksgiving. You've got to cheer up, though. I'm sure she'll be here for Christmas."*

"What are you doing?" Tanner asked, sounding testy again.

"Telling Butterpie that Sophie will be home at Christmas and she's got to cheer up in the meantime." He'd asked the question; let him deal with the answer.

"Are you crazy?"

"Probably," Olivia said. Then, speaking aloud this time, she told Butterpie, "I have to go now. I have a lost reindeer in the back of my Suburban, and I need to do some X-rays and then get him settled in over at my brother's place until I can find his owner. But I'll be back to visit soon, I promise."

She could almost hear Tanner grinding his back teeth.

"You should stand up," Olivia told the pony. "You'll feel better on your feet."

The animal gave a snorty sigh and slowly stood.

Tanner let out a sharp breath.

40

Olivia patted Butterpie's neck. "Excellent," she said. "That's the spirit."

"You have a reindeer in the back of your Suburban?" Tanner queried, keeping pace with Olivia as she left the barn.

"See for yourself," she replied, waving one hand toward the rig.

Tanner approached the vehicle, and Ginger barked a cheerful greeting as he passed the passenger-side window. He responded with a distracted wave, and Olivia decided there might be a few soft spots in his steely psyche after all.

Rubbing off dirt with one gloved hand, Tanner peered through the back windows.

"I'll be damned," he said. "It *is* a reindeer."

"Sure enough," Olivia said. Ginger was all over the inside of the rig, barking her brains out. She liked good-looking men, the silly dog. Actually, she liked *any* man. "Ginger! Sit!"

Ginger sat, but she looked like the poster dog for a homeless-pets campaign.

"Where did you get a reindeer?" Tanner asked, drawing back from the window to take a whole new look at Olivia.

Ridiculously, she wished she'd worn something remotely feminine that day, instead of her usual jeans, flannel work shirt and mud-speckled down-filled vest. Not that she actually owned anything remotely feminine.

"I found him," she said, opening the driver's door. "Last night, at the bottom of my driveway."

For the first time in their acquaintance, Tanner smiled, and the effect was seismic. His teeth were white and straight, and she'd have bet that was natural enamel, not a fancy set of veneers. "Okay," he said, stretching the word out a way. "Tell me, Dr. O'Ballivan — how does a reindeer happen to turn up in Arizona?"

"When I find out," Olivia said, climbing behind the wheel, "I'll let you know."

Before she could shut the door, he stood in the gap. Pushed his hat to the back of his head and treated her to another wicked grin. "I guess there's a ground-breaking ceremony scheduled for tomorrow morning at ten," he said. "I'll see you there."

Olivia nodded, feeling unaccountably flustered.

Ginger was practically drooling.

"Nice dog," Tanner said.

"Be still, my heart," Ginger said.

"Shut up," Olivia told the dog.

Tanner drew back his head, but the grin lurked in his eyes.

Olivia blushed. "I wasn't talking to you,"

she told Tanner.

He looked as though he wanted to ask if she'd been taking her medications regularly. Fortunately for him, he didn't. He merely tugged at the brim of his too-new hat and stepped back.

Olivia pulled the door closed, started up the engine, ground the gearshift into first and made a wide 360 in front of the barn.

"*That* certainly went well," she told Ginger. "We're going to be in each other's hip pockets while the shelter is being built, and he thinks I'm certifiable!"

Ginger didn't answer.

Half an hour later, the X-rays were done and the blood had been drawn. Rodney was good to go.

Tanner stood in the middle of the barnyard, staring after that wreck of a Suburban and wondering what the hell had just hit him. It felt like a freight train.

His cell phone rang, breaking the spell.

He pulled it from his jacket pocket and squinted at the caller ID panel. Ms. Wiggins, the executive principal at Briarwood. She'd certainly taken her time returning his call — he'd left her a message at sunrise.

"Tanner Quinn," he said automatically.

"Hello, Mr. Quinn," Ms. Wiggins said. A

43

former CIA agent, Janet Wiggins was attractive, if you liked the armed-and-dangerous type. Tanner didn't, particularly, but the woman had a spotless service record, and a good résumé. "I'm sorry I couldn't call sooner — meetings, you know."

"I'm worried about Sophie," he said. A cold wind blew down off the mountain looming above Stone Creek, biting into his ears, but he didn't head for the house. He just stood there in the barnyard, letting the chill go right through him.

"I gathered that from your message, Mr. Quinn," Ms. Wiggins said smoothly. She was used to dealing with fretful parents, especially the guilt-plagued ones. "The fact is, Sophie is not the only student remaining at Briarwood over the holiday season. There are several others. We're taking all the stay-behinds to New York by train to watch the Thanksgiving Day parade and dine at the Four Seasons. You would know that if you read our weekly newsletters. We send them by e-mail every Friday afternoon."

I just met a woman who talks to animals — and thinks they talk back.

Tanner kept his tone even. "I read your newsletters faithfully, Ms. Wiggins," he said. "And I'm not sure I like having my daughter referred to as a 'stay-behind.' "

Ms. Wiggins trilled out a very un-CIA-like giggle. "Oh, we don't use that term in front of the pupils, Mr. Quinn," she assured him. "Sophie is *fine.* She just tends to be a little overdramatic, that's all. In fact, I'm encouraging her to sign up for our thespian program, beginning next term —"

"You're sure she's all right?" Tanner broke in.

"She's one of our most emotionally stable students. It's just that, well, kids get a little sentimental around the holidays."

Don't we all? Tanner thought. He always skipped Thanksgiving and Christmas both, if he couldn't spend them with Sophie. Up until now it had been easy enough, given that he'd been out of the country last year, and the year before that. Sophie had stayed with Tessa, and he'd ordered all her gifts online.

Remembering that gave him a hollow feeling in the middle of his gut.

"I know Sophie is stable," he said patiently. "That doesn't mean she's completely okay."

Ms. Wiggins paused eloquently before answering. "Well, if you would like Sophie to come home for Thanksgiving, we'd certainly be glad to make the arrangements."

45

Tanner wanted to say yes. Instantly. *Book a plane. Put her on board. I don't care what it costs.* But it would only lead to another tearful parting when it came time for Sophie to return to school, and Tanner couldn't bear another one of those. Not just yet, anyway.

"It's best if Sophie stays there," he said.

"I quite agree," Ms. Wiggins replied. "Last-minute trips home can be very disruptive to a child."

"You'll let me know if there are any problems?"

"Of course I will," Ms. Wiggins assured him. If there was just a hint of condescension in her tone, he supposed he deserved it. "We at Briarwood pride ourselves on monitoring our students' mental health as well as their academic achievement. I promise you, Sophie is not traumatized."

Tanner wished he could be half as sure of that as Ms. Wiggins sounded. A few holiday platitudes were exchanged, and the call ended. Tanner snapped his phone shut and dropped it into his coat pocket.

Then he turned back toward the barn.

Could a horse get depressed?

Nah, he decided.

But a man sure as hell could.

■ ■ ■ ■

A snowman stood in the center of the yard at the homeplace when Olivia drove in, and there was one of those foldout turkeys taped to the front door. Brad came out of the barn, walking toward her, just as Meg, her sister-in-law, stepped onto the porch, smiling a welcome.

"How do you like our turkey?" she called. "We're really getting into the spirit this year." Her smile turned wistful. "It's strange, without Carly here, but she's having such a good time."

Grinning, Olivia gestured toward Brad. "He'll do," she teased.

Brad reached her, hooked an arm around her neck and gave her a big-brother half hug. "She's referring to the paper one," he told her in an exaggerated whisper.

Olivia contrived to look surprised. "Oh!" she said.

Brad laughed and released her from the choke hold. "So what brings you to Stone Creek Ranch, Doc?"

Olivia glanced around, taking in the familiar surroundings. Missing her grandfather, Big John, the way she always did when she set foot on home ground. The place had changed a lot since Brad had semiretired from his career in country music — he'd refurbished the barn, replaced the worn-out fences and built a state-of-the-art recording studio out back. At least he'd given up the concert tours, but even with Meg and fourteen-year-old Carly and the baby in the picture, Olivia still wasn't entirely convinced that he'd come home to stay.

He'd skipped out before, after all, just like their mother.

"I have a problem," she said in belated answer to his question.

Meg had gone back inside, but she and Brad remained in the yard.

"What sort of problem?" he asked, his eyes serious.

"A reindeer problem," Olivia explained. *Oh, and I got off to a fine start with your friend the contractor, too.*

Brad's brow furrowed. "A what?"

"I need to get out of this truck," Ginger transmitted from the passenger seat. *"Now."*

With a slight sigh Olivia opened Ginger's door so she could hop out, sniff the snow and leave a yellow splotch. That done, she trotted off toward the barn, probably looking for Brad's dog, Willie.

"I found this reindeer," Olivia said, heading for the back of the Suburban and unveiling Rodney. "I was hoping he could stay here until we find his owner."

"What if he doesn't have an owner?" Brad asked reasonably, running a hand through his shaggy blond hair before reaching out to stroke the deer.

"He's tame," Olivia pointed out.

"Tame, but not housebroken," Brad said.

Sure enough, Rodney had dropped a few pellets on his blanket.

"I don't expect you to keep him in the house," Olivia said.

Brad laughed. Reached right in and hoisted Rodney down out of the Suburban. The deer stumbled a little, wobbly legged from riding, and looked worriedly up at Olivia.

"You'll be safe here," she told the animal. She turned back to Brad. "He can stay in the barn, can't he? I know you have some empty stalls."

"Sure," Brad said after a hesitation that would have been comical if Olivia hadn't been so concerned about Rodney. "Sure," he repeated.

Knowing he was about to ruffle her hair, the way he'd done when she was a little kid, Olivia took a step back.

"I want something in return, though,"

Brad continued.

"What?" Olivia asked suspiciously.

"You, at our table, on Thanksgiving," he answered. "No excuses about filling in at the clinic. Ashley and Melissa are both coming, and Meg's mother, too, along with her sister, Sierra."

The invitation didn't come as any surprise to Olivia — Meg had mentioned holding a big Thanksgiving blowout weeks ago — but the truth was, Olivia preferred to work on holidays. That way, she didn't miss Big John so much, or wonder if their long-lost mother might come waltzing through the door, wanting to get to know the grown children she'd abandoned so many years before.

"Livie?" Brad prompted.

"Okay," she said. "I'll be here. But I'm on call over Thanksgiving, and all the other vets have families, so if there's an emergency —"

"Liv," Brad broke in, "*you* have a family, too."

"I meant wives, husbands, children," Olivia said, embarrassed.

"Two o'clock, you don't need to bring anything, and wear something you haven't delivered calves in."

She glared up at him. "Can I see my nephew now," she asked, "or is there a dress code for that, too?"

Brad laughed. "I'll get Rudolph settled in a nice, cozy stall while you go inside. Check the attitude at the door — Meg wasn't kidding when she said she was in the holiday spirit. Of course, she's working extra hard at it this year, with Carly away."

Willie and Ginger came from behind the barn, Willie rushing to greet Olivia.

"His name is Rodney," Olivia said. "Not Rudolph."

Brad gave her a look and started for the barn, and Rodney followed uncertainly, casting nary a backward glance at Olivia.

Willie, probably clued in by Ginger, was careful to give Rodney a lot of dog-free space. Olivia bent to scratch his ears.

He'd healed up nicely since being attacked by a wolf or coyote pack on the mountain rising above Stone Creek Ranch. With help from Brad and Meg, Olivia had brought him back to town for surgery and follow-up care. He'd bonded with Brad, though, and been his dog ever since.

With Ginger and Willie following, Olivia went into the house.

Mac's playpen stood empty in the living room.

Olivia stepped into the nearest bathroom to wash her hands, and when she came out,

51

Meg was standing in the hallway, holding six-month-old Mac. He stretched his arms out to Olivia and strained toward her, and her heart melted.

She took the baby eagerly and nuzzled his neck to make him laugh. His blondish hair stood up all over his head, and his dark blue eyes were round with mischievous excitement. Giggling, he tried to bite Olivia's nose.

"He's grown!" Olivia told Meg.

"It's only been a week since you saw him last," Meg chided, but she beamed with pride.

Olivia felt a pang, looking at her. Wondered what it would be like to be that happy.

Meg, blond like her husband and son, tilted her head to one side and gave Olivia a humorously pensive once-over. "Are you okay?" she asked.

"I'm fine," Olivia said, too quickly. Mac was gravitating toward his playpen, where he had a pile of toys, and Meg took him and gently set him inside it. She turned back to Olivia.

Just then Brad blew in on a chilly November wind. Bent to pat Ginger and Willie.

"Rudolph is snug in his stall," Brad said. "Having some oats."

"Rudolph?" Meg asked, momentarily distracted.

Olivia was relieved. She and Meg were very good friends, as well as family, but Meg was half again too perceptive. She'd figured out that something was bothering Olivia, and in another moment she'd have insisted on finding out what was up. Considering that Olivia didn't know that herself, the conversation would have been pointless.

"Liv will be here for Thanksgiving," Brad told Meg, pulling his wife against his side and planting a kiss on the top of her head.

"Of course she will," Meg said, surprised that there'd ever been any question. Her gaze lingered on Olivia, and there was concern in it.

Suddenly Olivia was anxious to go.

"I have two million things to do," she said, bending over the playpen to tickle Mac, who was kicking both feet and waving his arms, before heading to the front door and beckoning for Ginger.

"We'll see you tomorrow at the groundbreaking ceremony," Meg said, smiling and giving Brad an affectionate jab with one elbow. "We're expecting a big crowd, thanks to Mr. Country Music here."

Olivia laughed at the face Brad made, but then she recalled that Tanner Quinn would be there, too, and that unsettled feeling was back again. "The ground's pretty hard, thanks to the weather," she said, to cover the momentary lapse. "Let's hope Mr. Country Music still has the muscle to drive a shovel through six inches of snow and a layer of ice."

Brad showed off a respectable biceps, Popeye-style, and everybody laughed again.

"I'll walk you to the truck," he said, when Olivia would have ducked out without further ado.

He opened the driver's door of the Suburban, and Ginger made the leap, scrabbling across to the passenger seat. Olivia looked at her in surprise, since she usually wasn't that agile, but Brad reclaimed her attention soon enough.

"Is everything okay with you, Livie?" he asked. He and the twins were the only people in the world, now that Big John was gone, who called her Livie. It seemed right, coming from her big brother or her sisters, but it also made her ache for her grandfather. He'd loved Thanksgiving even better than Christmas, saying he figured the O'Ballivans had a great deal to be grateful for.

"Everything's fine," Olivia said. "Why does everybody keep asking me if I'm okay?

Meg did — now you."

"You just seem — I don't know — kind of sad."

Olivia didn't trust herself to speak, and suddenly her eyes burned with moisture.

Brad took her gently by the shoulders and kissed her on the forehead. "I miss Big John, too," he said. Then he waited while she climbed onto the running board and then the driver's seat. He shut the door and waved when she went to turn around, and when she glanced into the rearview mirror, he was still standing there with Willie, both of them staring after her.

CHAPTER THREE

Although Brad liked to downplay his success, especially now that he didn't go out on tour anymore, he was clearly still a very big deal. When Olivia arrived at the building site on the outskirts of Stone Creek at nine forty-five the next morning, the windswept clearing was jammed with TV news trucks and stringers from various tabloids. Of course the townspeople had turned out, too, happy that work was about to begin on the new animal shelter — and proud of their hometown boy.

Olivia's feelings about Brad's fame were mixed — he'd been away playing star when Big John needed him most, and she wasn't over that — but seeing him up there on the hastily assembled plank stage gave her a jolt of joy. She worked her way through the crowd to stand next to Meg, Ashley and Melissa, who were grouped in a little cluster up front, fussing over Mac. The baby's blue snowsuit was so bulky that he resembled the Michelin man.

Ashley turned to smile at Olivia, taking in her trim, tailored black pantsuit — a hold-over from her job interview at the veterinary clinic right after she'd finished graduate school. She'd ferreted through boxes until she'd found it, gone over the outfit with a lint roller to get rid of the ubiquitous pet hair, and hoped for the best.

"I guess you couldn't quite manage a dress," Ashley said without sarcasm. She was tall and blond, clad in a long skirt, elegant boots and a colorful patchwork jacket she'd probably whipped up on her sewing machine. She was also stubbornly old-fashioned — no cell phone, no Internet connection, no MP3 player — and Olivia had often thought, secretly of course, that her younger sister should have been born in the Victorian era, rather than modern times. She would have fit right into the 1890s, been completely comfortable cooking on a wood-burning stove, reading by gaslight and directing a contingent of maids in ruffly aprons and scalloped white caps.

"Best I could do on short notice," Olivia chimed in, exchanging a hello grin with Meg and giving Mac's mittened hand a little squeeze. His plump little cheek felt smooth and cold as she kissed him.

"Since when is a *year* 'short notice'?" Melissa put in, grinning. She and Ashley were fraternal twins, but except for their deep blue eyes, they bore no noticeable resemblance to each other. Melissa was small, an inch shorter than Olivia, and wore her fine chestnut-colored hair in a bob. Having left the law office where she worked to attend the ceremony, she was clad in her usual getup of high heels, pencil-straight skirt, fitted blazer and prim white blouse.

Up on stage, Brad tapped lightly on the microphone.

Everybody fell silent, as though the whole gathering had taken a single, indrawn breath all at the same time. The air was charged with excitement and civic pride and the welcome prospect of construction jobs to tide over the laid-off workers from the saw-mill.

Meg's eyes shone as she gazed up at her husband. "Isn't he something?" she marveled, giving Olivia a little poke with one elbow as she shifted Mac to her other hip.

Olivia smiled but didn't reply.

"Sing!" someone shouted, somewhere in the surging throng. Any moment now, Olivia thought, they'd all be holding up disposable lights in a flickering-flame salute.

Brad shook his head. "Not today," he said.

A collective groan rose from the crowd.

Brad put up both hands to silence them.

"He'll sing," Melissa said in a loud and certain whisper. She and Ashley, being the youngest, barely knew Brad. He'd been trying to remedy that ever since he'd moved back from Nashville, but it was slow going. They admired him, they were grateful to him, but it seemed to Olivia that her sisters were still in awe of their big brother, too, and therefore a strange shyness possessed them whenever he was around.

Brad asked Olivia and Tanner to join him on stage.

Even though Olivia had expected that, she wished she didn't have to go up there. She was a behind-the-scenes kind of person, uncomfortable at the center of attention. When Tanner appeared from behind her, took her arm and hustled her toward the wooden steps, she caught her breath. Stone Creekers raised an uproarious cheer, and Olivia flushed with embarrassment, but Tanner seemed untroubled.

He wore too-new, too-expensive boots, probably custom-made, to match his too-new hat, along with jeans, a black silk shirt and a denim jacket. He seemed as at home getting up in front of all those people as

Brad did — his grin dazzled, and his eyes were bright with enjoyment.

Drugstore cowboy, Olivia thought, but she couldn't work up any rancor. Tanner Quinn might be laying on the Western bit a little thick, but he did look good. Way, way too good for Olivia's comfort.

Brad introduced them both: Tanner as the builder, and Olivia — "You all know my kid sister, the horse doctor" — as the driving force behind the project. Without her, he said, none of this would be happening.

Never having thought of herself as a driving force behind anything in particular, Olivia grew even more flustered as Brad went on about how she'd be heading up the shelter when it opened around that time next year.

More applause followed, the good-natured, hometown kind, indulgent and laced with chuckles.

Let this be over, Olivia thought.

"Sing!" someone yelled. The whole audience soon took up the chant.

"Here's where we make a run for it," Tanner whispered to Olivia, and the two of them left the stage. Tanner vanished, and Olivia went back to stand with her sisters and Meg.

Brad grinned, shaking his head a little as

60

one of his buddies handed up a guitar. "One," he said firmly. After strumming a few riffs and turning the tuning keys this way and that, he eased into "Meg's Song," a ballad he'd written for his wife.

Holding Mac and looking up at Brad with an expression of rapt delight, Meg seemed to glow from the inside. A sweet, strange alchemy made it seem as though only Brad, Meg and Mac were really *there* during those magical minutes, on that blustery day, with the snow crusting hard around everybody's feet. The rest of them might have been hovering in an adjacent dimension, like actors waiting to go on.

When the song ended, the audience clamored for more, but Brad didn't give in. Photographers and reporters shoved in close as he handed off the guitar again, descended from the stage and picked up a brand-new shovel with a blue ribbon on the handle. The ribbon, Olivia knew, was Ashley's handiwork; she was an expert with bows, where Olivia always got them tangled up, fiddling with them until they were grubby.

"Are you making a comeback?" one reporter demanded.

"When will you make another movie?" someone else wanted to know.

Still another person shoved a microphone

into Brad's face; he pushed it away with a practiced motion of one arm. "We're here to break ground for an animal shelter," he said, and only the set of his jaw gave away the annoyance he felt. He beckoned to Olivia, then to Tanner, after glancing around to locate him.

Then, with consummate showmanship, Brad drove the shovel hard into the partially frozen ground. Tossed the dirt dangerously close to one reporter's shoes.

Olivia thought of the finished structure, and what it would mean to so many stray and unwanted dogs, cats and other critters, and her heart soared. That was the moment the project truly became real to her.

It was really going to happen.

There were more pictures taken after that, and Brad gave several very brief interviews, carefully steering each one away from himself and stressing the plight of animals. When one reporter asked if it wouldn't be better to build shelters for homeless *people,* rather than dogs and cats, Brad responded that compassion ought to begin at the simplest level, with the helpless, voiceless ones, and grow from there.

Olivia would have hugged her big brother in that moment if she'd been able to get close enough.

"Hot cider and cookies at my place," Ashley told her and Melissa. She was already heading for her funny-looking hybrid car, gleaming bright yellow in the wintry sunshine. "We need to plan what we're taking to Brad and Meg's for Thanksgiving dinner."

"I have to get back to work," Melissa said crisply. "Cook something and I'll pay you back." With that, she made for her spiffy red sports car without so much as a backward glance.

Olivia had rounds to make herself, though none of them were emergencies, and she had some appointments at the clinic scheduled for that afternoon, but when she saw the expression of disappointment on Ashley's face, she stayed behind. "I'll change clothes at your house," she said, and got into the Suburban to follow her sister back through town. Ginger had elected to stay home that day, claiming her arthritis was bothering her, and it felt odd to be alone in the rig.

Ashley's home was a large white Victorian house on the opposite side of Stone Creek, near the little stream with the same name. There was a white picket fence and plenty of gingerbread woodwork on the façade, and an ornate but tasteful sign stood in the snowy yard, bearing the words "Mountain View Bed-and-Breakfast" in elegant golden script. "Ashley O'Ballivan, Proprietor."

In summer, the yard burgeoned with colorful flowers.

But winter had officially come to the high country, and the blooming lilacs, peonies and English roses were just a memory. The day after Thanksgiving, the Christmas lights would go up outside, as though by the waving of an unseen wand, and a huge wreath would grace the leaded-glass door, making the house look like a giant greeting card.

Olivia felt a little sad, looking at that grand house. It was the off-season, and guests would be few and far between. Ashley would rattle around in there alone like a bean in the bottom of a bucket.

She needed a husband and children.

Or at least a cat.

"Brad was spectacular, wasn't he?" Ashley asked, bustling around her big, fragrant kitchen to heat up the spiced cider and set out a plate of exquisitely decorated cookies.

Olivia, just coming out of the powder room, where she'd changed into her regulation jeans, flannel shirt and boots, helped herself to a paper bag from the decoupaged wooden paper-bag dispenser beside the back door and stuffed the pantsuit into it.

"Brad was — Brad," she said. "He loves being in the limelight."

Ashley went still and frowned, oddly defensive. "His heart's in the right place," she replied.

Olivia went to Ashley and touched her arm. She'd removed the patchwork jacket, hanging it neatly on a gleaming brass peg by the front door as they came in, and her loose-fitting beige cashmere turtleneck made Olivia feel like a thrift-store refugee by comparison.

"I wasn't criticizing Brad, Ash," she said quietly. "It's beyond generous of him to build the shelter. We need one, and we're lucky he's willing to help out."

Ashley relaxed a little and offered a tentative smile. Looked around at her kitchen, which would have made a great set for some show on the Food Channel. "He bought this house for me, you know," she said as the cider began to simmer in its shiny pot on the stove.

Olivia nodded. "And it looks fabulous," she replied. "Like always."

"You *are* planning to show up for Thanksgiving dinner out at the ranch, aren't you?"

"Why wouldn't I?" Olivia asked, even as her stomach knotted. Who had invented holidays, anyway? Everything came to a screeching stop whenever there was a red-letter day on the calendar — everything except the need and sorrow that seemed to fill the world.

"I know you don't like family holidays," Ashley said, pouring steaming cider into a copper serving pot and then into translucent china teacups waiting in the center of the round antique table. Olivia would have dumped it straight from the kettle, and probably spilled it all over the table and floor in the process.

She just wasn't domestic. All those genes had gone to Ashley.

Her sister's eyes went big and round and serious. "Last year you made some excuse about a cow needing an appendectomy and ducked out before I could serve the pumpkin pie."

Olivia sighed. Ashley had worked hard to prepare the previous year's Thanksgiving dinner, gathering recipes for weeks ahead of time, experimenting like a chemist in search of a cure, and looked forward to hosting a houseful of congenial relatives.

"Do cows even *have* appendixes?" Ashley asked.

Olivia laughed, drew back a chair at the table and sat down. "That cider smells fabulous," she said, in order to change the subject. "And the cookies are works of art, almost too pretty to eat. Martha Stewart would be so proud."

Ashley joined her at the table, but she still looked troubled. "Why do you hate holidays, Olivia?" she persisted.

"I don't hate holidays," Olivia said. "It's just that all that sentimentality —"

"You miss Big John and Mom," Ashley broke in quietly. "Why don't you just admit it?"

"We all miss Big John," Olivia admitted. "As for Mom — well, she's been gone a long time, Ash. A *really* long time. It's not a matter of missing her, exactly."

"Don't you ever wonder where she went after she left Stone Creek, if she's happy and healthy — if she remarried and had more children?"

"I try not to," Olivia said honestly.

"You have abandonment issues," Ashley accused.

Olivia sighed and sipped from her cup of cider. The stuff was delicious, like everything her sister cooked up.

Ashley's Botticelli face brightened; she'd made another of her mercurial shifts from pensive to hopeful. "Suppose we found her?" she asked on a breath. "Mom, I mean —"

67

"Found her?" Olivia echoed, oddly alarmed.

"There are all these search engines on-line," Ashley enthused. "I was over at the library yesterday afternoon, and I searched Google for Mom's name."

Oh. My. God, Olivia thought, feeling the color drain out of her face.

"*You* used a computer?"

Ashley nodded. "I'm thinking of getting one. Setting up a Web site to bring in more business for the B and B."

Things were changing, Olivia realized. And she *hated* it when things changed. Why couldn't people leave well enough alone?

"There are more Delia O'Ballivans out there than you would ever guess," Ashley rushed on. "One of them must be Mom."

"Ash, Mom could be dead by now. Or going by a different name . . ."

Ashley looked offended. "You sound like Brad and Melissa. Brad just clams up whenever I ask him about Mom — he remembers her better, since he's older. 'Leave it alone' is all he ever says. And Melissa thinks she's probably a crack addict or a hooker or something." She let out a long, shaky breath. "I thought *you* missed Mom as much as I do. I really did."

Although Brad had never admitted it,

Olivia suspected he knew more about their mother than he was telling. If he wanted Ashley and the rest of them to let the proverbial sleeping dogs lie, he probably had a good reason. Not that the decision was only his to make.

"I miss *having* a mother, Ash," Olivia said gently. "That's different from missing Mom specifically. She left us, remember?"

Remember? How *could* Ashley remember? She'd been a toddler when their mother boarded an afternoon bus out of Stone Creek and vanished into a world of strangers. She was clinging to memories she'd merely imagined, most likely. To a fantasy mother, the woman who should have been, but probably never was.

"Well, I want to know why," Ashley insisted, her eyes full of pain. "Maybe she regretted it. Did you ever think of that? Maybe she misses us, and wants a second chance. Maybe she expects us to reject her, so she's afraid to get in touch."

"Oh, Ash," Olivia murmured, slouching against the back of her chair. "You haven't actually made contact, have you?"

"No," Ashley said, tucking a wisp of blond hair behind her right ear when it escaped from her otherwise categorically perfect French braid, "but if I find her, I'm going to invite her to Stone Creek for Christmas. If you and Brad and Melissa want to keep your distance, that's your business."

Olivia's hand shook a little as she set her cup down, causing it to rattle in its delicate saucer. "Ashley, you have a right to see Mom if you want to," she said carefully. "But Christmas —"

"What do you care about Christmas?" Ashley asked abruptly. "You don't even put up a tree most years."

"I care about you and Melissa and Brad. If you do manage to find Mom, great. But don't you think bringing her here at Christmas, the most emotional day of the year, before anybody has a chance to get used to the idea, would be like planting a live hand grenade in the turkey?"

Ashley didn't reply, and after that the conversation was stilted, to say the least. They talked about what to contribute to the Thanksgiving shindig at Brad and Meg's place, decided on freshly baked dinner rolls for Ashley and a selection of salads from the deli for Olivia, and then Olivia left to make rounds.

Why was she so worried? she wondered, biting down hard on her lower lip as she fired up the Suburban and headed for the first farm on her list. If she was alive, Delia

70

had done a good job of staying under the radar all these years. She'd never written, never called, never visited. Never sent a single birthday card. And if she was dead, they'd all have to drop everything and mourn, in their various ways.

Olivia didn't feel ready to take that on.

Before, the thought of Delia usually filled her with grief and a plaintive, little-girl kind of longing. The very cadence of her heartbeat said, *Come home. Come home.*

Now, today, it just made her very, very angry. How could a woman just leave four children and a husband behind and forget the way back?

Olivia knotted one hand into a fist and bonked the side of the steering wheel once. Tears stung her eyes, and her throat felt as though someone had run a line of stitches around it with a sharp needle and then pulled them tight.

Ashley was expecting some kind of fairytale reunion, an *Oprah* sort of deal, full of tearful confessions and apologies and cartoon birds trailing ribbons from their chirpy beaks.

For Olivia's money, it would be more like an apocalypse.

Tanner heard the rig roll in around sunset.

71

Smiling, he closed his newspaper, stood up from the kitchen table and wandered to the window. Watched as Olivia O'Ballivan climbed out of her Suburban, flung one defiant glance toward the house and started for the barn, the golden retriever trotting along behind her.

She'd come, he knew, to have another confab with Butterpie. The idea at once amused him and jabbed through his conscience like a spike. Sophie was on the other side of the country, homesick as hell and probably sticking pins in a daddy doll. She missed the pony, and the pony missed her, and *he* was the hard-ass who was keeping them apart.

Taking his coat and hat down from the peg next to the back door, he put them on and went outside. He was used to being alone, even liked it, but keeping company with Doc O'Ballivan, bristly though she sometimes was, would provide a welcome diversion.

He gave her time to reach Butterpie's stall, then walked into the barn.

The golden came to greet him, all wagging tail and melting brown eyes, and he bent to stroke her soft, sturdy back. "Hey, there, dog," he said.

Sure enough, Olivia was in the stall,

brushing Butterpie down and talking to her in a soft, soothing voice that touched something private inside Tanner and made him want to turn on one heel and beat it back to the house.

He'd be damned if he'd do it, though.

This was *his* ranch, *his* barn. Well-intentioned as she was, *Olivia* was the trespasser here, not him.

"She's still very upset," Olivia told him without turning to look at him or slowing down with the brush.

For a second Tanner thought she was referring to Sophie, not the pony, and that got his hackles up.

Shiloh, always an easy horse to get along with, stood contentedly in his own stall, munching away on the feed Tanner had given him earlier. Butterpie, he noted, hadn't touched her supper as far as he could tell.

"Do you know anything at all about horses, Mr. Quinn?" Olivia asked.

He leaned against the stall door, the way he had the day before, and grinned. He'd practically been raised on horseback; he and Tessa had grown up on their grandmother's farm in the Texas hill country, after their folks divorced and went their separate ways, both of them too busy to bother with a couple of kids. "A few things," he said. "And I mean to call you Olivia, so you might as well return the favor and address me by my first name."

He watched as she took that in, dealt with it, decided on an approach. He'd have to wait and see what that turned out to be, but he didn't mind. It was a pleasure just watching Olivia O'Ballivan grooming a horse.

"All right, *Tanner,*" she said. "This barn is a disgrace. When are you going to have the roof fixed? If it snows again, the hay will get wet and probably mold. . . ."

He chuckled, shifted a little. He'd have a crew out there the following Monday morning to replace the roof and shore up the walls — he'd made the arrangements over a week before — but he felt no particular compunction to explain that. He was enjoying her ire too much; it made her color rise and her hair fly when she turned her head, and the faster breathing made her perfect breasts go up and down in an enticing rhythm. "What makes you so sure I'm a greenhorn?" he asked mildly, still leaning on the gate.

At last she looked straight at him, but she didn't move from Butterpie's side. "Your hat, your boots — that fancy red truck you drive. I'll bet it's customized."

Tanner grinned. Adjusted his hat. "Are you telling me real cowboys don't drive red trucks?"

"There are lots of trucks around here," she said. "Some of them are red, and some of them are new. And *all* of them are splattered with mud or manure or both."

"Maybe I ought to put in a carwash, then," he teased. "Sounds like there's a market for one. Might be a good investment."

She softened, though not significantly, and spared him a cautious half smile, full of questions she probably wouldn't ask. "There's a good car wash in Indian Rock," she informed him. "People go there. It's only forty miles."

"Oh," he said with just a hint of mockery. "*Only* forty miles. Well, then. Guess I'd better dirty up my truck if I want to be taken seriously in these here parts. Scuff up my boots a bit, too, and maybe stomp on my hat a couple of times."

Her cheeks went a fetching shade of pink. "You are twisting what I said," she told him, brushing Butterpie again, her touch gentle but sure. "I meant . . ."

Tanner envied that little horse. Wished he had furry hide, so he'd need brushing, too.

"You *meant* that I'm not a real cowboy,"

75

he said. "And you could be right. I've spent a lot of time on construction sites over the last few years, or in meetings where a hat and boots wouldn't be appropriate. Instead of digging out my old gear, once I decided to take this job, I just bought new."

"I bet you don't even *have* any old gear," she challenged, but she was smiling, albeit cautiously, as though she might withdraw into a disapproving frown at any second.

He took off his hat, extended it to her. "Here," he teased. "Rub that around in the muck until it suits you."

She laughed, and the sound — well, it caused a powerful and wholly unexpected shift inside him. Scared the hell out of him and, paradoxically, made him yearn to hear it again. "That would be a little drastic," she said.

Tanner put his hat back on. "You figure me for a rhinestone cowboy," he said. "What else have you decided about me?"

She considered the question, evidently drawing up a list in her head.

Tanner was fascinated — and still pretty scared.

"Brad told me you were widowed," she said finally, after mulling for a while. "I'm sorry about that."

Tanner swallowed hard, nodded. Won-

76

dered how much detail his friend had gone into, and decided not to ask. He'd told Brad the whole grim story of Kat's death, once upon a time.

"You're probably pretty driven," Olivia went on, concentrating on the horse again. "It's obvious that you're successful — Brad wouldn't have hired you for this project if you weren't the best. And you compartmentalize."

"Compartmentalize?"

"You shut yourself off from distractions."

"Such as?"

"Your daughter," Olivia said. She didn't lack for nerve, that was for sure. "And this poor little horse. You'd like to have a dog — you like Ginger a lot — but you wouldn't adopt one because that would mean making a commitment. Not being able to drop everything and everybody and take off for the next Big Job when the mood struck you."

Tanner felt as though he'd been slapped, and it didn't help one bit that everything she'd said was true. Which didn't mean he couldn't deny it.

"I *love* Sophie," he said grimly.

She met his gaze again. "I'm sure you do. Still, you find it easy enough to — compartmentalize where she's concerned, don't you?"

"I do not," he argued. He *did* "compartmentalize" — he had to — but he sure as hell wouldn't call it easy. Every parting from Sophie was harder on him than it was on her. He was the one who always had to suck it up and be strong.

Olivia shrugged, patted the pony affectionately on the neck and set aside the brush. "I'll be back tomorrow," she told the animal. "In the meantime, think good thoughts and talk to Shiloh if you get too lonesome."

Tanner racked his brain, trying to remember if he'd told Olivia the gelding's name. He was sure it hadn't come up in their brief but tempestuous acquaintance. "How did you . . . ?"

"He told me," Olivia said, approaching the stall door and waiting for him to step out of her way, just like before.

"Are you seriously telling me I've got Mr. Ed in my barn?" he asked, moving aside so she could pass.

She crossed to Shiloh's stall, reached up to stroke his nose when he nuzzled her and gave a companionable nicker. "You wouldn't understand," she said, with so much smug certainty that Tanner found himself wanting to prove a whole bunch of things he'd never felt the need to prove before.

"Because I compartmentalize?" Tanner gibed.

"Something like that," Olivia answered blithely. She turned from Shiloh, snapped her fingers to attract the dog's attention and started for the barn door.

"See you tomorrow, if you're here when I come by to look in on Butterpie."

Utterly confounded, Tanner stood in the doorway watching as Olivia lowered a ramp at the back of the Suburban for Ginger, waited for the dog to trot up it, and shut the doors.

Moments later she was driving off, tooting a merry "so long" on the horn.

That night he dreamed of Kat.

She was alive again, standing in the barn at Butterpie's stall gate, watching as the pony nibbled hay at its feeder. Tall and slender, with long dark hair, Kat turned to him and smiled a welcome.

He hated these dreams for *being* dreams, not reality. At the same time he couldn't bring himself to wake up, to leave her.

The settings were always different — their first house, their quarters in the American compound in some sandy, dangerous foreign place, even supermarket aisles and gas stations. He'd be standing at the pump, filling the vehicle *de jour,* and look up to see Kat with a hose in her hand, gassing up that old junker she'd been driving when they met.

He stood at a little distance from her, there in the barn aisle, well aware that after a few words, a few minutes at most, she'd vanish. And it would be like losing her all over again.

She smiled, but there was sadness in her eyes, in the set of her full mouth. "Hello, Tanner," she said very softly.

He couldn't speak. Couldn't move. Somehow he knew that this visit was very different from all the ones that had gone before.

She came to stand in front of him, soft as summer in her white cotton sundress, and touched his arm as she looked up into his face.

"It's time for me to move on," she told him.

No.

The word swelled up inside him, but he couldn't say it.

And Kat vanished.

CHAPTER FOUR

Olivia awakened on the following Thursday morning feeling as though she hadn't slept at all the night before, with Ginger's cold muzzle pressed into her neck and the alarm clock buzzing insistently. She stirred, opened her eyes, slapped down the snooze button, with a muttered "Shut *up!*"

Iridescent frost embossed the window glass in intricate fans and swirls, turning it opaque, but the light got through anyway, signaling the arrival of a new day — like it or not.

Thanksgiving, Olivia recalled. *The official start of the holiday season.*

She groaned and yanked the covers up over her head.

Ginger let out an impatient little yip.

"I know," Olivia replied from under two quilts and a flannel sheet worn to a delectable, hard-to-leave softness. It was so warm under those covers, so cozy. Would that she could stay right there until sometime after the Second Coming. "I know you need to go outside."

Ginger yipped again, more insistently this time.

Bleary-eyed, Olivia rolled onto her side, tossed back the covers and sat up. She'd slept in gray sweats and heavy socks — less than glamorous attire, for sure, but toasty and loose.

After hitting the stop button on the clock so it wouldn't start up again in five minutes, she stumbled out of the bedroom and down the hall toward the small kitchen at the back of the house. Passing the thermostat, she cranked it up a few degrees. As she groped her way past the coffeemaker, she jabbed blindly at yet another button to start the pot she'd set up the night before. At the door she shoved her feet into an old pair of ugly galoshes and shrugged into a heavy jacket of red-and-black-plaid wool — Big John's chore coat.

It still smelled faintly of his budget aftershave and pipe tobacco.

The weather stripping stuck when she tried to open the back door, and she muttered a four-letter word as she tugged at the knob. The instant there was a crack to pass through, Ginger shot out of that kitchen like a clown dog from a circus cannon. She banged open the screen door beyond, too, without slowing down for the enclosed porch.

"Ginger!" Olivia yelled, startled, before taking one rueful glance back at the coffee-maker. It shook and gurgled like a miniature rocket trying to lift off the counter, and it would take at least ten minutes to produce enough java to get Olivia herself off the launch pad. She needed to buy a new one — item number seventy-two on her domestic to-do list. The timer had given out weeks ago, and the handle on the carafe was loose.

And where the hell was the dog headed? Ginger *never* ran.

Olivia shook the last clinging vestiges of sleep out of her head and tromped through the porch and down the outside steps, taking care not to slip on the ice and either land on her tailbone or take a flyer into the snowbank beside the walk.

"Ginger!" she called a second time as the dog streaked halfway down the driveway, shinnied under the rail fence between Olivia's place and Tanner's and bounded out into the snowy field.

Goose-stepping it to the fence, Olivia climbed onto the lowest rail and shaded her eyes from the bright, cold sun. What was

83

Ginger chasing? Coyotes? Wolves? Either way, that was a fight an aging golden retriever couldn't possibly win.

Olivia was about to scramble over the fence and run after the dog when she saw the palomino in the distance, and the man sitting tall in the saddle.

Tanner.

The horse moved at a smooth trot while Ginger cavorted alongside, flinging up snow, like a pup in a superchow commercial.

Olivia sighed, partly out of relief that Ginger wasn't about to tangle with the resident wildlife and partly because Tanner was clearly headed her way.

She looked down at her rumpled sweats; they were clean, but the pants had worn threadbare at the knees and there was a big bleach stain on the front of the shirt. She pulled the front of Big John's coat closed with one hand and ran the other through her uncombed hair.

Tanner's grin flashed as white as the landscape around him when he rode up close to the fence. Despite the grin, he looked pale under his tan, and there was a hollow look in his eyes. The word *haunted* came to mind.

"Mornin', ma'am," he drawled, tugging at

the brim of his hat. "Just thought I'd mosey on over and say howdy."

"How very Western of you," Olivia replied with a reluctant chuckle.

Ginger, winded by the unscheduled run, was panting hard.

"What in the world got into you?" Olivia scolded the dog. "Don't you ever do that again!"

Ginger crossed the fence line and slunk toward the house.

When Olivia turned back to Tanner, she caught him looking her over.

Wise guy.

"It would be mighty neighborly of you to offer a poor wayfaring cowboy a hot cup of coffee," he said. He sat that horse as if he was part of it — a point in his favor. He might dress like a dandy, but he was no stranger to a saddle.

"Glad to oblige, mister," Olivia joked, playing along. "Unless you insist on talking like a B-movie wrangler for much longer. That could get old."

He laughed at that, rode to the rickety gate a few yards down the way, leaned to work the latch easily and joined Olivia on her side. Taking in the ramshackle shed and detached garage, he swung down out of the saddle to walk beside her, leading Shiloh by a slack rein.

"Looks to me like you don't have a whole lot of room to talk about the state of my barn," he said. His eyes were twinkling now under the brim of his hat, though he still looked wan.

It was harder going for Olivia — her legs were shorter, the galoshes didn't fit so they stuck at every step, and the snow came to her shins. "I rent this place," she said, feeling defensive. "The owner lives out of state and doesn't like to spend a nickel on repairs if he can help it. In fact, he's been threatening to sell it for years."

"Ah," Tanner said with a sage nod. "Are you just passing through Stone Creek, Doc? I had the impression you were a lifelong resident, but maybe I was wrong."

"Except for college and veterinary school," Olivia answered, "I've lived here all my life." She looked around at the dismal rental property. "Well, not right here —"

"Hey," Tanner said, quietly gruff. "I was kidding."

She nodded, embarrassed because she'd been caught caring what he thought, and led the way through the yard toward the back door.

Tanner left Shiloh loosely tethered to the hand rail next to the porch steps.

Inside the kitchen, Olivia fed a remorseful Ginger, washed her hands at the sink and got two mugs down out of the cupboard. The coffeemaker was just flailing in for a landing, mission accomplished.

"Excuse me for a second, will you?" Olivia asked after filling mugs for herself and Tanner and giving him his. She slipped into the bedroom, closed the door, put down her coffee cup and quickly switched out the chore coat and her sweats for her best pair of jeans and the blue sweater Ashley had knitted for her as a Christmas gift. She even went so far as to splash her face with water in the tiny bathroom, give her teeth a quick brushing and run a comb through her hair.

When she returned to the kitchen, Tanner was sitting in a chair at the table, looking as if he belonged there, and Ginger stood with her head resting on his thigh while he stroked her back.

Something sparked in Tanner's weary eyes when he looked up — maybe amusement, maybe appreciation. Maybe something more complicated.

Olivia felt a wicked little thrill course through her system.

"Thanksgiving," she said without planning to, almost sighing out the word.

"You don't sound all that thankful,"

87

Tanner observed.

"Oh, I am," Olivia insisted, taking a sip from her mug.

"Me, too," Tanner said. "Mostly."

She bit her lower lip, stole a glance at the clock above the sink. It was early — two hours before she needed to check in at the clinic. So much for excusing herself to go to work.

"Mostly?" she echoed, keeping her distance.

"There are things I'd change about my life," Tanner told her. "If I could."

She drew nearer then, interested in spite of herself, and sat down, though she kept the width of the table between them. "What would you do differently?"

He sighed, and a bleak expression darkened his eyes. "I'd have kept the business smaller, for one thing," he said. The briefest flicker of pain contorted his face. "Not gone international. How about you?"

"I'd have spent more time with my grandfather," she replied after giving the question some thought. "I guess I figured he was going to be around forever."

"That was his coat you were wearing before."

"How did you guess that?"

"My grandmother had one just like it. I

88

think they must have sold those at every farm supply store in America, back in the day."

Olivia relaxed a little. "How's Butterpie?"

Tanner sighed, met Olivia's gaze. Held it. "She's not eating," he said.

"I was afraid of that," Olivia murmured, distracted.

"I thought my grandmother was going to live forever, too," Tanner told her.

It took Olivia a moment to catch up. "She's gone, then?"

Tanner nodded. "Died on her seventy-eighth birthday, hoeing the vegetable garden. Just the way she'd have wanted to go — quick, and doing something she loved to do. Your grandfather?"

"Heart attack," Olivia said, running her palms along the thighs of her jeans. Why were they suddenly moist?

Tanner was silent for what seemed like a long time, though it was an easy silence. Then he finished his coffee and stood. "Guess I'd better not keep you," he said, crossing the room to set his cup in the sink.

Ginger's liquid eyes followed him adoringly.

"I'd like to look in on Butterpie on my way into town, if that's okay with you?" Olivia said.

One side of Tanner's fine mouth slanted slightly upward. "Would it stop you if it *wasn't* okay with me?"

She grinned. "Nope."

He chuckled at that. "I've got some things to do in town," he said. "Gotta pick up some wine for Thanksgiving dinner. So if I don't see you in my barn, we'll meet up at Brad and Meg's place later on."

Of *course* her brother and sister-in-law would have invited Tanner to join them for Thanksgiving dinner. He was a friend, and he lived alone. Still, Olivia felt blindsided. Holidays were hard enough without stirring virtual strangers into the mix. Especially *attractive* ones.

"See you then," she said, hoping her smile didn't look forced.

He nodded and left, closing the kitchen door quietly behind him. Olivia immediately went to the window to watch him mount Shiloh and ride off.

When he was out of sight, and only then, Olivia turned from the window and zeroed in on Ginger.

"What were you *thinking,* running off like that? You're not a young dog, you know."

"I just got a little carried away, that's all," Ginger said without lifting her muzzle off her forelegs. Her eyes looked soulful. *"Are*

90

you wearing that getup to Thanksgiving dinner?"

Olivia looked down at her jeans and
sweater. "What's wrong with my outfit?" she
asked.

*"Touchy, touchy. I was just asking a simple
question."*

"These jeans are almost new, and Ashley
made the sweater. I look perfectly fine."

"Whatever you say."

"Well, what do *you* think I should wear, O
fashionista dog?"

"The sweater's fine," Ginger observed. *"But
I'd switch out the jeans for a skirt. You do have
a skirt, don't you?"*

"Yes, I have a skirt. I also have rounds to
make before dinner, so I'm changing into
my work clothes right now."

Ginger sighed an it's-no-use kind of sigh.
"Paris Hilton you ain't," she said, and drifted
off to sleep.

Olivia returned to her bedroom, put on
her normal grubbies, suitable for barns and
pastures, then located her tan faux-suede
skirt, rolled it up like a towel and stuffed it
into a gym bag. Knee boots and the blue
sweater went in next, along with the one
pair of panty hose she owned. They had
runs in them, but the skirt was long and the
boots were high, so it wouldn't matter.

91

When she got back to the kitchen, Ginger was stretching herself.

"You're coming with me today, aren't you?" Olivia asked.

Ginger eyed the gym bag and sighed again. *"As far as next door, anyway,"* she answered. *"I think Butterpie could use some company."*

"What about Thanksgiving?"

"Bring me a plate," Ginger replied.

Oddly disappointed that Ginger didn't want to spend the holiday with her, Olivia went outside to fire up the Suburban and scrape off the windshield. After she'd lowered the ramp in the back of the rig, she went back to the house for Ginger.

"You're all right, aren't you?" Olivia asked as Ginger walked slowly up the ramp.

"I'm not used to running through snow up to my chest," the dog told her. *"That's all."*

Still troubled, Olivia stowed the ramp and shut the doors on the Suburban. Ginger curled up on Rodney's blanket and closed her eyes.

When they arrived at Tanner's place, his truck was parked in the driveway, but he didn't come out of the house, and Olivia didn't knock on the front door. She repeated the ramp routine, and then she and Ginger headed into the barn.

Shiloh was back in his stall, brushed down and munching on hay.

Olivia paused to greet him, then opened the door to Butterpie's stall so she and Ginger could go in.

Butterpie stood with her head hanging low, but perked up slightly when she saw the dog.

"You've got to eat," Olivia told the pony.

Butterpie tossed her head from side to side, as though in refusal.

Ginger settled herself in a corner of the roomy stall, on a pile of fresh wood shavings, and gave another big sigh. *"Just go make your rounds,"* she said to Olivia. *"I'll get her to take a few bites after you're gone."*

Olivia felt bereft at the prospect of leaving Ginger and the pony. She found an old pan, filled it with water at the spigot outside, returned to set it down on the stall floor. "This is weird," she said to Ginger. "What's Tanner going to think if he finds you in Butterpie's stall?"

"That you're crazy," Ginger answered. *"No real change in his opinion."*

"Very funny," Olivia said, not laughing. Or even smiling. "You're sure you'll be all right? I could come back and pick you up before I head for Stone Creek Ranch."

Ginger shut her eyes and gave an eloquent snore.

After that, there was no point in talking to her.

Olivia gave Butterpie a quick but thorough examination and left.

Tanner bought a half case of the best wine he could find — Stone Creek had only one supermarket, and the liquor store was closed. He should have lied, he thought as he stood at the checkout counter, paying for his purchases. Told Brad he had plans for Thanksgiving.

He was going to feel like an outsider, passing a whole afternoon and part of an evening with somebody else's family.

Better that, though, he supposed, than eating alone in the town's single sit-down restaurant, remembering Thanksgivings of old and missing Kat and Sophie.

Kat.

"Is that good?" the clerk asked.

Distracted, Tanner didn't know what the woman was talking about at first. Then she pointed to the wine. She was very young and very pretty, and she didn't seem to mind working on Thanksgiving when practically everybody else in the western hemisphere was bellying up to a turkey feast

94

someplace.

"I don't know," Tanner said in belated answer to her cordial question. He'd been something of a wine aficionado once, but since he didn't indulge anymore, he'd sort of lost the knack. "I go by the labels, and the price."

The clerk nodded as if what he'd said made a lick of sense, and wished him a happy Thanksgiving.

He wished her the same, picked up the wine box, the six bottles rattling a little inside it, and made for the door.

The dream came back to him, full force, as he was setting the wine on the passenger seat of his truck.

Kat, standing in the aisle of the barn, in that white summer dress, telling him she wouldn't be back.

It was no good telling himself he'd only been dreaming in the first place. He'd held on to those night visits — they'd gotten him through a lot of emotional white water. It had been Kat who'd said he ought to watch his drinking. Kat who'd advised him to accept the Stone Creek job and oversee it himself instead of sending in somebody else.

Kat who'd insisted the newspapers were wrong; she hadn't been a target — she'd been caught in the cross fire of somebody else's fight. Sophie, she'd sworn, was in no danger.

She'd faded before his eyes like so much thin smoke a couple of nights before. The wrench in his gut had been powerful enough to wake up him up. The dream had stayed with him, though, which was the same as having it over and over again. Last night he'd been unable to sleep at all. He'd paced the dark empty house for a while, then, unable to bear it any longer, he'd gone out to the barn, saddled Shiloh and taken a moonlight ride.

For a while he'd tried to outride what he was feeling — not loss, not sorrow, but a sense of letting go. Of somehow being set free.

He'd *loved* Kat, more than his own life. Why should her going on to wherever dead people went have given him a sense of liberation, even exaltation, rather than sorrow?

The guilt was almost overwhelming. As long as he'd mourned her, she'd seemed closer somehow. Now the worst was over. There had been some kind of profound shift, and he hadn't regained his footing.

They'd been out for hours, he and Shiloh, when he was crossing the field between his place and Olivia's and that dog of hers came racing toward him. He'd have gone home, put Shiloh up with some extra grain for his trouble, taken a shower and fallen into bed if it hadn't been for Ginger and the sight of Olivia standing on the bottom rail of the fence.

She'd been wearing sweats and silly rubber boots and an old man's coat, and for all that, she'd managed to look sexy. He'd finagled an invitation for coffee — hell, he'd flat out invited *himself* — and thought about taking her to bed the whole time he was there.

Not that he would have made a move on Doc. It was way too soon, and she'd probably have conked him over the head with the nearest heavy object, but he'd been tempted, just the same.

Tempted as he'd never been, since Kat.

At home he left the wine in the truck and headed for the barn.

Shiloh was asleep, standing up, the way horses do. When Tanner looked over the stall door at Butterpie, though, his eyes started to sting. Butterpie was lying in the wood shavings, and Olivia's dog was cuddled up right alongside her, as though keeping some kind of a vigil.

"I'll be damned," Tanner muttered. He'd grown up in the country, and he'd known

horses to have nonequine companions —
cows, cats, dogs and even pygmy goats. But
he'd never seen anything quite like this.

He figured he probably should take Ginger
home — Olivia might be looking for her —
but he couldn't quite bring himself to part
the two animals.

"You hungry, girl?" he asked Ginger,
thinking what a fine thing it would be to
have a dog. The problem was, he moved
around too much — job to job, country to
country. If he couldn't raise his own daughter, how could he hope to take good care of
a mutt?

Ginger made a low sound in her throat
and looked up at him with those melty eyes
of hers. He made a quick trip into the house
for a hunk of cube steak and a bowl of
water, and set them both down where she
could reach them.

She drank thirstily of the water, nibbled at
the steak.

Tanner patted her head. He'd seen her
jump into Olivia's Suburban the day before,
so she still had some zip in her, despite the
gray hairs around her muzzle, but she
hadn't gotten over that stall door by herself.
Olivia must have left her here, to look after
the pony.

When he spotted an old grain pan in the

corner, overturned, he knew that was what had happened. She must have found the pan in the junk around the barn, filled it with water and left it so the dog could drink. Then one of the animals, most likely Butter-pie, had stepped on the thing and spilled the contents.

He was pondering that sequence of events when his cell phone rang.

Sophie.

"This parade bites," she said without any preamble. "It's cold, and Mary Susan Parker keeps sneezing on me and we're not allowed to get into the minibar in our hotel suite! Ms. Wiggins took the keys away."

Tanner chuckled. "Hello and happy Thanksgiving to you, too, sweetheart," he said, so glad to hear her voice that his eyes started stinging again.

"It's not like we want to drink *booze* or anything," Sophie complained. "But we can't even help ourselves to a soda or a candy bar!"

"Horrible," Tanner commiserated.

An annoyed silence crackled from Sophie's end.

"Butterpie has a new friend," Tanner said, to get the conversation going again. In a way, talking to Sophie made him miss her more, but at the same time he wanted to keep her on the line as long as possible. "A dog named Ginger."

He'd caught Sophie's interest that time. "Really? Is it your dog?"

It was telling, Tanner thought, that Sophie had said "your dog" instead of "our dog." "No. Ginger lives next door. She's just here for a visit."

"I'm lonely, Dad," Sophie said, sounding much younger than her twelve years. She was almost shouting to be heard over a brass band belting out "Santa Claus Is Coming to Town." "Are you lonely, too?"

"Yes," he replied. "But there are worse things than being lonely, Soph."

"Right now I can't think of any. Are you going to be all alone all day?"

Crouching now, Tanner busied himself scratching Ginger's ears. "No. A friend invited me to dinner."

Sophie sighed with apparent relief. "Good. I was afraid you'd nuke one of those frozen TV dinners or something and eat it while you watched some football game. And that would be *pathetic.*"

"Far be it from me to be pathetic," Tanner said, but a lump had formed in his throat and his voice came out sounding hoarse. "Anything but that."

"What friend?" Sophie persisted. "What

friend are you having dinner with, I mean?"

"Nobody you know."

"A woman?" Was that *hope* he heard in his daughter's voice? "Have you met someone, Dad?"

Damn. It *was* hope. The kid probably fantasized that he'd remarry one day, and she could come home from boarding school for good, and they'd all live happily ever after, with a dog and two cars parked in the same garage every night, like a normal family.

That was never going to happen.

Ginger looked up at him in adoring sympathy when he rubbed his eyes, tired to the bone. His sleepless night was finally catching up with him — or that was what he told himself.

"No," he said. "I haven't met anybody, Soph." Olivia's face filled his mind. "Well, I've met somebody, but I haven't *met* them, if you know what I mean."

Sophie, being Sophie, *did* know what he meant. Exactly.

"But you're dating!"

"No," Tanner said quickly. Bumming a cup of coffee in a woman's kitchen didn't constitute a date, and neither did sitting at the same table with her on Thanksgiving Day. "No. We're just — just friends."

"Oh." Major disappointment. "This whole thing bites!"

"So you said," Tanner replied gently, wanting to soothe his daughter but not having the first clue how to go about it. "Maybe it's your mind-set. Since today's Thanksgiving, why not give gratitude a shot?"

She hung up on him.

He thought about calling her right back, but decided to do it later, after she'd had a little time to calm down, regain her perspective. She was a lucky kid, spending the holiday in New York, watching the famous parade in person, staying in a fancy hotel suite with her friends from school.

"Women," he told Ginger.

She gave a low whine and laid her muzzle on his arm.

He stayed in the barn a while, then went into the house, took a shower, shaved and crashed, asleep before his head hit the pillow.

And Kat did not come to him.

Olivia had stopped by Tanner's barn on the way to Stone Creek Ranch, hoping to persuade Ginger to take a break from horse-sitting, but she wouldn't budge.

Arriving at the homeplace, she checked on Rodney, who seemed content in his stall, then, gym bag in hand, she slipped inside the small bath off the tack room and grabbed a quick, chilly shower. She shimmied into those wretched panty hose, donned the skirt and the blue sweater and the boots, and even applied a little mascara and lip gloss for good measure.

Never let it be said that she'd come to a family dinner looking like a — *veterinarian.*

And the fact that Tanner Quinn was going to be at this shindig had absolutely *nothing* to do with her decision to spruce up.

Starting up the front steps, she had a sudden, poignant memory of Big John standing on that porch, waiting for her to come home from a high school date with Jesse McKettrick. After the dance all the kids had gone to the swimming hole on the Triple M, and splashed and partied until nearly dawn.

Big John had been furious, his face like a thundercloud, his voice dangerously quiet.

He'd given Jesse what-for for keeping his granddaughter out all night, and grounded Olivia for a month.

She'd been outraged, she recalled, smiling sadly. Tearfully informed her angry grandfather that *nothing had happened* between her and Jesse, which was true, if you didn't count necking. Now, of course, she'd have given almost anything to see that temperamental old man again, even if he *was* shaking his finger at her and telling her that in his day, young ladies knew how to behave themselves.

Lord, how she missed him, missed his rants. *Especially* the rants, because they'd been proof positive that he cared what happened to her.

The door opened just then, and Brad stepped out onto the porch, causing the paper turkey to flutter on its hook behind him.

"Ashley's going to kill me," Olivia said. "I forgot to pick up salads at the deli."

Brad laughed. "There's so much food in there, she'll never know the difference. Now, come on in before we both freeze to death."

Olivia hesitated. Swallowed. Watched as Brad's smile faded.

"What is it?" he asked, coming down the steps.

"Ashley's looking for Mom," she said. She hadn't planned to bring that up that day. It just popped out.

"What?"

"She's probably going to announce it at dinner or something," Olivia rushed on. "Is it just me, or do you think this is a bad idea, too?"

"It's a very bad idea," Brad said.

"You know something about Mom, don't you? Something you're keeping from the rest of us." It was a shot in the dark, a wild guess, but it struck the bull's-eye, dead center. She knew that by the grim expression on Brad's famous face.

"I know enough," he replied.

"I shouldn't have brought it up, but I was thinking about Big John, and that led to thinking about Mom, and I remembered what Ashley told me, so —"

"It's okay," Brad said, trying to smile. "Maybe she won't bring it up."

Olivia doubted they could be that lucky. Ashley was an O'Ballivan through and through, and when she got on a kick about something, she had to ride it out to the bitter end. "I could talk to her . . ."

Brad shook his head, pulled her inside the house. It was too hot and too crowded and too loud, but Olivia was determined to make the best of the situation, for her family's sake, if not her own.

Big John would have wanted it that way.

She hunted until she found Mac, sitting up in his playpen, and lifted him into her arms. "It smells pretty good in here, big guy," she told him. There was a fragrant fire crackling on the hearth, and Meg had lit

105

some scented candles, and delicious aromas wafted from the direction of the kitchen.

Out of the corner of her eye Olivia spotted Tanner Quinn standing near Brad's baby grand piano, dressed up in a black suit, holding a bottle of water in one hand and trying hard to look as though he was enjoying himself.

Seeing his discomfort took Olivia's mind off her own. Still carrying Mac, she started toward him.

A cell phone went off before she could speak to him — *How the Grinch Stole Christmas* — and Tanner immediately reached into his pocket. Flipped open the phone.

As Olivia watched, she saw the color drain out of his face.

The water bottle slipped, and he caught it before it fell, though barely.

"What's wrong?" Olivia asked.

Mac, perfectly happy a moment before that, threw back his head and wailed for all he was worth.

"My daughter," Tanner said, standing stock-still. "She's gone."

CHAPTER FIVE

This was the call Tanner had feared since the day Kat died. Sophie, gone missing — or worse. Now that it had actually happened, he seemed to be frozen where he stood, fighting a crazy compulsion to run in all directions at once.

Olivia handed off the baby to Brad, who'd appeared at her side instantly, and touched Tanner's arm. "What do you mean, she's gone?"

Before he could answer, the cell ran through its little ditty again.

He didn't bother checking the caller ID panel. "Sophie?"

"Jack McCall," his old friend said. "We found Sophie, buddy. She's okay, if a little — make that a lot — disgruntled."

Relief washed over Tanner like a tidal wave, making him sway on his feet. "She's really all right?" Jack had been there for Tanner when Kat was killed, and if there was a blow coming, he might try to soften it.

Olivia stood looking up at him, waiting, her hand still resting lightly on his arm, fingers squeezing gently.

"She's *fine*," Jack said easily. "Like I said, she's not real happy about being nabbed, though."

"Where was she?" Tanner had to feel around inside his muddled brain for the question, thrust it out with force.

"Grand Central," Jack answered. "She sneaked away from the school group while they were making their way through the crowds after the parade. Fortunately, one of my guys spotted her right away, and tailed her to the station. She was buying a train ticket west."

Coming home. Sophie had been trying to come home.

Brad pulled out the piano bench, and Tanner sat down heavily, tossing his friend a grateful glance.

"Question of the hour," Jack went on. "What do we do now? She swears she'll run away again if we take her back to school, and I believe her. The kid is serious, Tanner."

Tanner let out a long sigh. He felt sick, light-headed, imagining all the things that could have happened to Sophie. And very, very glad when Olivia sat down on the bench beside him, her shoulder touching his. "Can you bring her here?" he asked. "To Stone Creek?"

"I'll come with her as far as Phoenix," Jack said. "I'll have my people there bring her the rest of the way by helicopter. The jet's due in L.A. by six o'clock Pacific time, and it's a government job, high-security south-of-the-border stuff, so I can't get out of the gig."

Tanner glanced sidelong at Olivia. She took his hand and clasped it. "I appreciate this, Jack," he said into the phone, his voice hoarse with emotion. "Send Sophie home."

Olivia smiled at that. Brad let out a sigh, grinned and went back to playing host at a family Thanksgiving dinner, taking his son with him. Folks started milling toward the food, laid out buffet-style in the dining room.

"Ten-four, old buddy," Jack said. "Maybe I'll stop in out there and say hello on my way back from Señoritaville. Book me a room somewhere, will you? I could do with a few months of R & R."

A few minutes before, Tanner couldn't have imagined laughing, ever again. But he did then. "That would be good," he said, choking up again. "Your being here, I mean. I'll ask around, find you a place to stay."

"Adios, amigo," Jack told him, and rang off.

"Sophie's okay?" Olivia asked softly.

"Until I get my hands on her, she is," Tanner answered.

"Stay right here," Olivia said, rising and taking off for the dining room beyond.

A short time later she was back, carrying two plates. "You need to eat," she informed Tanner.

And that was how they shared Thanksgiving dinner, sitting on Brad O'Ballivan's piano bench, with the living room all to themselves and blessedly quiet. Tanner was surprised to discover that he wasn't just hungry, he was ravenous.

"Feeling better?" Olivia asked when he was finished.

"Yeah," he answered. "But I don't think I'm up to socializing all afternoon."

"Me, either," Olivia confessed. She'd only picked at her food.

"Is there a sick cow somewhere?" Tanner asked, indulging in a slight grin. After the shock Sophie had given him, he was still pretty shaken up. "That would probably serve as an excuse for getting the heck out of here."

"They're all ridiculously healthy today," Olivia said.

Tanner chuckled. "Sorry to hear that," he teased.

She laughed, but the amusement didn't quite get as far as her eyes. Tanner wondered why the holiday made her so uncomfortable, but he didn't figure he knew her well enough to ask. He knew why *he* didn't like them — because the loss of his wife and grandmother stood out in sharp relief against all that merriment. And maybe that was Olivia's reason, too.

"I *am* pretty concerned about Butterpie," she said, as if inspired. "What do you say we steal one of the fifty-eight pumpkin pies lining Meg's kitchen counter and head back to your barn?"

Maybe it was the release of tension. Maybe it was because Olivia looked and smelled so damn good — almost as good as she had that morning, out by the fence and then later on, in her kitchen. Either way, the place he wanted to take her wasn't his barn.

"Okay," he said. "But if you're caught pie-napping, I'll deny being in cahoots with you."

Again that laugh, soft and musical and utterly feminine. It rang in Tanner's brain, then lodged itself square in the center of his heart. "Fair enough," she said.

She took their plates and left again, making for the kitchen.

Tanner found Brad standing by the sideboard in the big dining room, affably directing traffic between the food and the long table, where there was a lot of happy talk and dish clattering going on.

"Everything okay, buddy?" Brad asked, watching Tanner's face.

"I got a little scare," Tanner answered, shoving a hand through his hair. He knew a number of famous people, and not one of them was as down-home and levelheaded as Brad O'Ballivan. He was a man who had more than enough of everything, and knew it, and lived a comparatively simple life. "Just the same, I need a little alone time."

Brad nodded. Caught sight of Olivia coming out of the kitchen with the purloined pie and small plastic container, stopping to speak to Meg as she passed the crowded table. His gaze swung right back to Tanner. "Alone time, huh?" he asked.

"It's not what you think," Tanner felt compelled to say, feeling some heat rise in his neck.

Brad arched an eyebrow. Regarded him thoughtfully. "You're a good friend," he said. "But I love my sister. Keep that in mind, all right?"

Tanner nodded, liking Brad even more than before. Look out for the womenfolk — it was the cowboy way. "I'll keep it in mind," he replied.

He and Olivia left Stone Creek Ranch at the same time, he in his too-clean red truck, she in that scruffy old Suburban. The drive to Starcross took about fifteen minutes, and Olivia was out of her rig and headed into the barn before he'd parked his pickup.

Butterpie was on her feet, Ginger rising from a stretch when Tanner caught up to Olivia in front of the stall door. Olivia opened the plastic container, revealing leftover turkey.

"Tell Butterpie Sophie's coming home," he said, without intending to say any such thing.

Olivia smiled, inside the stall now, letting Ginger scarf up cold turkey from the container. "I already did," she replied. "That's why Butterpie is up. She could use a little exercise, so let's turn her out in the corral for a while."

Tanner nodded, found a halter and slipped it over Butterpie's head. Led her outside and over to the corral gate, and turned her loose.

Olivia and Ginger stood beside him,

watching as the pony looked around, as if baffled to find herself outside in the last blaze of afternoon sunlight and the heretofore pristine snow. The dog barked a couple of times, as if to encourage Butterpie.

Tanner shook his head. Ridiculous, he thought. Dogs didn't *encourage* horses.

He recalled finding Ginger huddled close to Butterpie in the stall earlier in the day. Or *did* they?

Butterpie just stood there for a while, then nuzzled through the snow for some grass.

Whether the little horse had cheered up or not, *he* certainly had. Butterpie hadn't eaten anything since she'd arrived at Starcross Ranch, and now she was ready to graze. He went back into the barn and came out with a flake of hay, tossed it into the corral.

Butterpie nosed it around a bit and began to nibble.

Olivia watched for a few moments, then turned to Tanner and took smug note of the hay stuck to the front of his best suit. "You might be a real cowboy after all," she mused, and that simple statement, much to Tanner's amazement, pleased him almost as much as knowing Sophie was safe with his best friend, Jack McCall.

"Thanks," he said, resting his arms on the

top rail of the corral fence and watching Butterpie eat.

When the pony came to the gate, clearly ready to return to the barn, Tanner led her back to her stall and got her settled in. Olivia and Ginger followed, waiting nearby.

"So what happened with Sophie?" Olivia asked when Tanner came out of the stall.

"I'll explain it over coffee and pie," he said, holding his figurative breath for her answer. If Olivia decided to go home, or make rounds or something, he was going to be seriously disappointed.

"This place used to be wonderful," Olivia said, minutes later, when they were in his kitchen, with the coffee brewing and the pie sitting on the table between them.

Tanner wished he'd taken down the old calendar, spackled the holes in the wall from the tacks that had held up its predecessors. Replaced the flooring and all the appliances, and maybe the cupboards, too. The house still looked abandoned, he realized, even with him living in it.

What did *that* mean?

"I'll fix it up," he said. "Sell it before I move on." It was what he always did. Buy a house, keep a careful emotional distance from it, refurbish it and put it on the market, always at a profit.

115

Something flickered in Olivia's eyes. Seeing that *he'd* seen, she looked away, though not quickly enough.

"Did you know the previous owner well?" he asked, to get her talking again. The sound of her voice soothed him, and right then he needed soothing.

"Of course," she said, turning the little tub of whipped cream, stolen along with the pie and the leftovers for Ginger, in an idle circle on the tabletop. "Clarence was one of Big John's best friends. He was widowed sometime in the mid-nineties — Clarence, I mean — and after that he just lost interest in Starcross." She paused, sighed, a small frown creasing the skin between her eyebrows. "He got rid of the livestock, cow by cow, horse by horse. He stopped doing just about everything." Another break came then. "It's the name, I think."

"The name?"

"Of the ranch," Olivia clarified. "Starcross. It's — sad."

Tanner found himself grinning a little. "What would you call it, Doc?" he asked. The coffee was finished, and he got up to find some cups and pour a dose for both of them.

She considered his question as if there

were really a name change in the offing. "Something, well, *happier,*" she said as he set the coffee down in front of her, realized they'd need plates and forks for the pie and went back to the cupboards to rustle some up. "More positive and cheerful, I guess, like The Lucky Horseshoe, or The Diamond Spur. Something like that."

Tanner had no intention of giving the ranch a new name — why go to all the trouble when he'd be leaving in a year at the longest? — but he enjoyed listening to Olivia, watching each new expression cross her face. The effect was fascinating.

And oh, that face.

The body under it was pretty spectacular, too.

Tanner shifted uncomfortably in his chair.

"Don't you think those names are a little pretentious?" he asked, cutting into the pie.

"Corny, maybe," Olivia admitted, smiling softly. "But not pretentious."

He served her a piece of pie, then cut one for himself. Watched with amusement and a strange new tenderness as she spooned on the prepackaged whipped cream. She looked pink around the neck, perhaps a little discomforted because he was staring.

He averted his eyes, but a moment later

he was looking again. He couldn't seem to help it.

"You took the first chance you could get to bolt out of that Thanksgiving shindig at your brother's place," he said carefully. "Why is that, Doc?"

"Why do you keep calling me 'Doc'?" She *was* nervous, then. Maybe she sensed that Tanner wanted to kiss her senseless and then take her upstairs to his bed.

"Because you're a doctor?"

"I have a name."

"A very beautiful name."

She grinned, and some of the tension eased, which might or might not have been a good thing. "Get a shovel," she said. "It's getting deep in here."

He laughed, pushed away his pie.

"I should go now," she said, but she looked and sounded uncertain.

Hallelujah, Tanner thought. She was tempted, at least.

"Or you could stay," he suggested casually.

She gnawed at her lower lip. "Is it just me?" she asked bluntly. "Or are there sexual vibes bouncing off the walls?"

"There are definitely vibes," he confirmed.

"We haven't even kissed."

"That would be easy to remedy."

"And we've only known each other a few days."

"We're both adults, Olivia."

"I can't just — just go to bed with you, just because I —"

"Just because you want to?"

Challenge flared in her eyes, and she straightened her shoulders.

"Who says I want to?"

"Do you?"

"Yes," she said, after a very long time. Then, quickly, "But that doesn't mean I will."

"Of course it doesn't."

"People ought to say no to themselves once in a while," she went on, apparently grasping at moral straws. "This society is way too into instant gratification."

"I promise you," Tanner said drily, "it won't be instant."

Color flooded her face, and he could see her pulse beating hard at the base of her throat.

"When was the last time you made love?" he asked when she didn't say anything. Nor, to his satisfaction, did she jump to her feet and bolt for the door.

Tanner's hopes were rising, and so was something else.

"That's a pretty personal question," she

119

said, sounding miffed. She even went so far as to glance over at the dog, sleeping the sleep of the innocent on the rug in front of the stove.

"I'll tell if you will."

"It's been a while," she admitted loftily. "And maybe I don't *want* to know who you've had sex with and how recently. Did that ever occur to you?"

"A while as in six months to a year, or never?"

"I'm not a virgin, if that's what you're trying to find out."

"Good," he said.

"I'm leaving," she said. But she didn't get up from her chair. She didn't call the dog, or even put down her fork, though she wasn't taking in much pie.

"You're free to do that."

"Of course I am."

"*Or* we could go upstairs, right now."

She swallowed visibly, and her wonderful eyes widened.

Hot damn, she was actually considering it.

Letting herself go. Doing something totally irresponsible, just for the hell of it. Tanner went hard, and he was glad she couldn't see through the tabletop.

"No strings attached?" she asked.

"No strings," Tanner promised, though he felt a little catch inside, saying the words. He wondered at his reaction, but not for long.

He was a man, after all, sitting across a table from one of the loveliest, most confusing women he'd ever met.

"I suppose we're just going to obsess until we do it," Olivia said. Damn, but she was full of surprises. He'd expected her to be talking herself *out* of going to bed with him, not *into* it.

"Probably," Tanner said, very seriously.

"Get it out of the way."

"Out of our systems," Tanner agreed, wanting to keep the ball rolling. Watching for the right time to make his move and all the time asking himself what the hell he was doing.

He stood up.

She stood up. And probably noticed his erection.

Would she run for it after all?

Tanner waited.

She waited.

"Can I kiss you?" he asked finally. "We could decide after that."

"Good idea," Olivia said, but her pulse was still fluttering visibly, at her temple now as well as her throat, and her breathing was quick and shallow, raising and lowering her breasts under that soft blue sweater.

She didn't move, so it fell to Tanner to step in close, take her face in his hands and kiss her, very gently at first, then with tongue.

What was she *doing?* Olivia fretted, even as she stood on tiptoe so Tanner could kiss her more deeply. Sure, it had been a while since she'd had sex — ten months, to be exact, with the last man she'd dated — but it wasn't as if she were *hot to trot* or anything like that.

This . . . *this* was like storm chasing — venturing too close to a tornado and getting sucked in by the whirlwind. She felt both helpless and all-powerful, standing there in Tanner Quinn's dreary kitchen — helpless because she'd known even before they left Stone Creek Ranch that this would happen, and all powerful because *damn it,* she wanted it, too.

She wanted hot, sticky, wet *sex.* And she knew Tanner could give it to her.

They kissed until her knees felt weak, and she sagged against Tanner.

Then he lifted her into his arms. "You're sure about this, Doc?"

She swallowed, nodded. "I'm sure."

Ginger raised her head, lowered it again and went back to sleep.

His room was spacious and relatively clean, though he probably hadn't made the bed since he'd moved in. Olivia noted these things with a detached part of her brain, but her elemental, primitive side wanted to rip off her clothes as if they were on fire.

Tanner undressed her slowly, kissing her bare shoulder when he unveiled it, then her upper breast. When he tongued her right nipple, then her left, she gasped and arched her back, wanting more.

He stopped long enough to shed his suit coat and toss aside his tie.

Olivia handled the buttons and buckle and finally the zipper.

And they were both naked.

He kissed her again, eased her down on the side of the bed, knelt on the floor to kiss her belly and her thighs. "Where's the whipped cream when you need it?" he teased, his voice a low rumble against her flesh.

"Oh, God," Olivia said, because she knew what he was going to do, and because she wanted so much for him to do it.

He burrowed through the nest of curls at the apex of her thighs, found her with his mouth, suckled, gently at first, then greedily.

He made a low sound to let her know he was enjoying her, but she barely heard it over the pounding of her heart and the creaking of the bed springs as her hips rose and fell in the ancient dance.

He slid his hands under her, raised her high off the bed and feasted on her in earnest. The first orgasm broke soon after that, shattering and sudden, and so long that Olivia felt as though she were being tossed about on the head of a fiery geyser.

Just when she thought she couldn't bear the pleasure for another moment — or live without it — he allowed her to descend. She marveled at his skill even as she bounced between one smaller, softer climax after another.

At last she landed, sated and dazed, and let out a croony sigh.

She heard the drawer on the bedside stand open and close.

"Still sure?" Tanner asked, shifting his body to reach for what he needed.

She nodded. Gave another sigh. "Oh, very sure," she said.

He turned her on the bed, slipped a pillow under her head and kissed her lightly. She clasped her hands behind his head and pulled him closer, kissed him back.

This part was for him, she thought magnanimously. She'd had her multiclimax — now it was time to be generous, let Tanner enjoy the satisfaction he'd earned.

Oh, God, had he earned it.

Except that when he eased inside her, she was instantly aroused, every cell in her body screaming with need. She couldn't do it; she couldn't come like that a second time without disintegrating — could she?

She was well into the climb, though, and there was no going back.

They shared the next orgasm, and the one after that.

And then they slept.

It was dark in the room when Olivia awakened, panic-stricken, to a strange whuff-whuff-whuff sound permeating the roof of that old house. Tanner was nowhere to be seen.

She flew out of bed, scrambled into her clothes, except for the panty hose, which she tossed into the trash — what *was* that deafening noise? — and dashed down the back stairs into the kitchen. Ginger, on her feet and barking, paused to give her a knowing glance.

"Shut up," Olivia said, hurrying to the window.

Tanner was out there, standing in what appeared to be a floodlight, looking up. Then the helicopter landed, right there in the yard.

Olivia rubbed her eyes hard, but when she looked again, the copter was still there, black and ominous against the snow. The blades slowed and then a young girl got out of the bird, stood still. Tanner stooped as he went toward the child, put an arm around her shoulders and steered her away, toward the house.

He paused when the copter lifted off again, waved.

Sophie had arrived, Olivia realized. And in grand style, too.

"Do I look like I've just had sex?" she asked Ginger in a frantic whisper.

"I wouldn't know what you look like when you've just had sex," Ginger answered. *"I'm a dog, remember?"*

"Before you start yelling at me," Sophie said, looking up at Tanner with Kat's eyes, "can I just say hello to Butterpie?"

Tanner, torn between wishing he believed in spanking kids and a need to hold his daughter safe and close and tight, shoved his hands into the pockets of his leather jacket. "The barn's this way," he said,

126

though it was plainly visible, and started walking.

Sophie shivered as she hurried along beside him. "We could," she said breathlessly, "just dispense with the yelling entirely and go on from there."

"Fat chance," Tanner told her.

"I'm in trouble, huh?"

"What do you think?" Tanner retorted, trying to sound stern. In truth, he was so glad to see Sophie, he hardly trusted himself to talk.

He should have woken Olivia when he got the call from Jack's pilot, he thought. Warned her of Sophie's impending arrival.

As if she could have missed hearing that helicopter.

"I think," Sophie said with the certainty of youth, "I'm really happy to be here, and if you yell at me, I can take it."

Tanner suppressed a chuckle. This was no time to be a pal. "You could have been kidnapped," he said. "The list of things that might have happened to you —"

"*Might* have," Sophie pointed out sagely. "That's the key phrase, Dad. Nothing *did* happen, except one of Uncle Jack's guys collared me at Grand Central. *That* was a tense moment, not to mention embarrassing."

Having made that statement, Sophie

dashed ahead of him and into the barn, calling Butterpie's name.

By the time he flipped on the overhead lights, she was already in the stall, hugging the pony's neck.

Butterpie whinnied with what sounded like joy.

And Olivia appeared at Tanner's elbow. "We'll be going now," she said quietly, watching the reunion with a sweet smile. "Ginger and I."

"Wait," Tanner said when she would have turned away. "I want you to meet Sophie."

"This is your time, and Sophie's," Olivia said, standing on tiptoe to kiss his cheek. "Tomorrow, maybe."

It was a simple kiss, nothing compared to the ones they'd shared upstairs in his bedroom. Just the same, Tanner felt as though he'd stepped on a live wire. His skeleton was probably showing, like in a cartoon.

"Maybe you feel like explaining what I'm doing here at this hour," she reasoned, with a touch of humor lingering on her mouth, "but I don't."

Reluctantly Tanner nodded.

Ginger and Olivia left, without Sophie ever noticing them.

■ ■ ■ ■

At home, Olivia showered, donned a ragged chenille bathrobe and listened to her voice mail, just in case there was an emergency somewhere. She'd already checked her cell phone, but you never knew.

The only message was from Ashley. "Where *were* you?" her younger sister demanded. "Today was *Thanksgiving!*"

Olivia sighed, waited out the diatribe, then hit the bullet and pressed the eight key twice to connect with Ashley.

"Mountain View Bed-and-Breakfast," Ashley answered tersely. She already knew who was calling, then. Hence the tone.

"Any openings?" Olivia asked, hoping to introduce a light note.

Ashley wasn't biting. She repeated her voice mail message, almost verbatim, ending with another "Where were you?"

"There was an emergency," Olivia said. What else could she say? *I was in bed with Tanner Quinn and I had myself a hell of a fine time, thank you very much.*

Suspicion, tempered by the knowledge that emergencies were a way of life with Olivia. "What kind of emergency?"

Olivia sighed. "You don't want to know,"

she said. It was true, after all. Ashley was a normal, healthy woman, but that didn't mean she'd want a blow-by-blow description — so to speak — of what she and Tanner had done in his bed.

"Another cow appendectomy?" Ashley asked, half sarcastic, half uncertain.

"A clandestine operation," she said, remembering the black helicopter. *That* would give the local conspiracy theorists something to chew on for a while, if they'd seen it.

"Really? There was an operation?"

Tanner was certainly an operator, Olivia thought, so she said yes.

"And here I thought you were probably having sex with that contractor Brad hired to build the shelter," Ashley said with an exasperated little sigh.

Olivia swallowed a giggle. Spoke seriously. "Ashley O'Ballivan, why would you think a thing like that?"

"Because I saw you leave with him," Ashley answered. Her tone turned huffy again. "I wanted to tell Brad and Melissa that I've decided to look for Mom," she complained. "And I couldn't do it without you there."

Olivia sobered. "Pretty heavy stuff, when Brad and Meg had a houseful of guests, wouldn't you say?"

Ashley went quiet again.

"Ash?" Olivia prompted. "Are you still there?"

"I'm here."

"So why the sudden silence?"

Another pause. A long one that gave Olivia plenty of time to worry. Then, finally, the bomb dropped. "I think I've already found her."

CHAPTER SIX

"This place," Sophie said, looking around at the ranch-house kitchen the next morning, "needs a woman's touch. Or maybe a crack decorating crew from HGTV or DIY."

Tanner, still half-asleep, stood at the counter pouring badly needed coffee. Between Sophie's great adventure and all that sex with Olivia, he felt disoriented, out of step with his normal world. "You watch HGTV and DIY?" he asked after taking a sip of java to steady himself.

"Doesn't everybody?" Sophie countered. "I've been thinking of flipping houses when I grow up." She looked so much like her mother, with her long, shiny hair and expressive eyes. Right now those eyes held a mixture of trepidation, exuberance and sturdy common sense.

"Trust me," Tanner said, treading carefully, finding his way over uncertain ground, because they weren't really talking about real estate and he knew it. "Flipping houses is harder than a thirty-minute TV show makes it seem."

"You should know," Sophie agreed airily, taking in the pitiful kitchen again. "You'll manage to turn this one over for a big profit, though, just like all the others."

Tanner dragged a chair back from the table and sort of fell into it. "Sit down, Soph," he said. "We've got more important things to discuss than the lineup on your favorite TV channels."

Sophie crossed the room dramatically and dropped into a chair of her own. She'd had the pajamas she was wearing now stashed in her backpack, which showed she'd been planning to ditch the school group in New York, probably before she left Briarwood. Now she was playing it cool.

Tanner thought of Ms. Wiggins's plans to steer her into the thespian program at school, and stifled a grimace. His sister, Tessa, had been a show-business kid, discovered when she did some catalog modeling in Dallas at the age of eight. She'd done commercials, guest roles and finally joined a long-running hit TV series. As far as he was concerned, that had been the wrong road. It was as though Tessa — wonderful, smart, beautiful Tessa — had peaked at twenty-one, and been on a downhill slide ever since.

"You're mad because I ran away," Sophie said, sitting up very straight, like a witness taking the stand. She seemed to think good posture might sway the judge to decide in her favor. In any case, she was still acting.

"Mad as hell," Tanner agreed. "That was a stupid, dangerous thing to do, and don't think you're going to get away with it just because I'm so glad to see you."

The small face brightened. "*Are* you glad to see me, Dad?"

"Sophie, of course I am. I'm your father. I miss you a lot when we're apart."

She sighed and shut off the drama switch. Or at least dimmed it a little. "Most of the time," she said, "I feel like one of those cardboard statues."

Tanner frowned, confused. "Run that by me again?"

"You know, those life-size depictions you see in the video store sometimes? Johnny Depp, dressed up like Captain Jack, or Kevin Costner like Wyatt Earp, or something like that?"

Tanner nodded, but he was still pretty confounded. There was nothing two-dimensional about Sophie — she was 3-D all the way.

But did she know that?

"It's as if I'm made of cardboard as far as you're concerned," she went on thoughtfully. "When I'm around, great. When I'm not, you just tuck me away in a closet to gather dust until you want to get me out again."

Tanner's gut clenched, hard. And his throat went tight. "Soph —"

"I know you don't really think of me that way, Dad," his daughter broke in, imparting her woman-child wisdom. "But it *feels* as if you do. That's all I'm saying."

"And I'm saying I don't want you to feel that way, Soph. Ever. All I'm doing is trying to keep you safe."

"I'd rather be happy."

Another whammy. Tanner got up, emptied his cup at the sink and nonsensically filled it up again. Stood with his back to the counter, leaning a little, watching his daughter and wondering if all twelve-year-olds were as complicated as she was.

"You'll understand when you're older," he ventured.

"I understand *now*," Sophie pressed, and she looked completely convinced. "You're the bravest man I know — you were Special Forces in the military, with Uncle Jack — but you're scared, too. You're scared I'll get

135

hurt because of what happened to Mom."

"You can't possibly remember that very well."

Benevolent contempt. "I was *seven,* Dad. Not two." She paused, and her eyes darkened with pain. "It was awful. I kept thinking, *This can't be real, my mom can't be gone,* but she was."

Tanner went to his daughter, laid a hand on top of her head, too choked up to speak.

Sophie twisted slightly in the chair, so she could look up at him. "Here's the thing, Dad. Bad things happen to people. Good people, like you and me and Mom. You have to cry a lot, and feel really bad, because you can't help it, it hurts so much. But then you've got to go on. Mom wouldn't want us living apart like we do. I *know* she wouldn't."

He thought of the last dream-visit from Kat, and once again felt a cautious sense of peace rather than the grief he kept expecting to hit him. He also recalled the way he'd abandoned himself in Olivia's arms the day before, in his bed, and a stab of guilt pricked his conscience, small and needle sharp.

"Your mother," he said firmly, "would want what's best for you. And that's getting a first-rate education in a place where you can't be hurt."

"Get real, Dad," Sophie scoffed. "I could

136

get hurt *anywhere,* including Briarwood."

Regrettably, that was true, but it was a whole lot less likely in a place he'd designed himself. The school was a fortress.

Or was it, as Sophie had said more than once, a prison?

You had to take the good with the bad, he decided.

"You're going back to Briarwood, kiddo," he said.

Sophie's face fell. "I could be a big help around here," she told him.

The desperation in her voice bruised him on the inside, but he had to stand firm. The stakes were too high.

"Can't I just stay until New Year's?" she pleaded.

Tanner sighed. "Okay," he said. "New Year's. Then you *have to go back.*"

"What about Butterpie?" Sophie asked, always one to press an advantage, however small. "Admit it. She hasn't been doing very well without me."

"She can go with you," Tanner said, deciding the matter as the words came out of his mouth. "It's time Briarwood had a stable, anyway. Ms. Wiggins has been hinting for donations for the last year."

"I guess that's better than a kick in the pants," Sophie said philosophically. Where

137

did she *get* this stuff?

In spite of himself, Tanner laughed. "It's my best offer, shorty," he said. "Take it or leave it."

"I'll take it," Sophie said, being nobody's fool. "But that doesn't mean I won't try to change your mind in the meantime."

Tanner opened the refrigerator door, ferreted around for the makings of a simple breakfast. If he hadn't been so busy rolling around in the sack with Olivia yesterday afternoon, he thought, he'd have gone to the grocery store. Stocked up on kid food.

Whatever that was.

"Try all you want," he said. "My mind is made up. Go get dressed while I throw together an omelet."

"Yes, sir!" Sophie teased, standing and executing a pretty passable salute. She raced up the back stairs, presumably to rummage through her backpack, the one piece of luggage she'd brought along, for clothes. Tanner simultaneously cracked eggs and juggled the cordless phone to call Tessa.

His sister answered on the third ring, and she sounded disconsolate but game. "Hello, Tanner," she said.

No matter how she felt, Tessa always tried to be a good sport and carry on. It was a trait they shared, actually, a direct dispensation from their unsinkable grandmother, Lottie Quinn.

"Hey," he responded, whipping the eggs with a fork, since he hadn't bothered to ship his kitchen gear to Stone Creek and there was no whisk. He was going to have to go shopping, he realized, for groceries, for household stuff and for all the things Sophie would need.

Shopping, on the busiest day of the retail year.

The thought did not appeal.

"How's Sophie?" Tessa asked, with such immediacy that for a moment Tanner thought she knew about the Great Escape. Then he realized that Tessa worried about the kid as much as he did. She disapproved of Briarwood, referring to him as an "absentee father," which never failed to get under his hide and nettle like a thorn. But she worried.

"She's here for Christmas," he said, as though he'd planned things to turn out that way. They'd need a tree, too, and lights, he reflected with half his mind, and all sorts of those hangy gewgaws to festoon the branches. Things were getting out of hand, fast, now that Hurricane Sophie had made landfall. "Why don't you join us?"

"Nobody to watch the horses," Tessa replied.

"You okay?" Tanner asked, knowing she wasn't and wishing there was one damned thing he could do about it besides wait and hope she'd tell him if she needed help. There were probably plenty of people to look after Tessa's beloved horses — most of her friends were equine fanatics, after all — but she didn't like to ask for a hand.

Another joint inheritance from Lottie Quinn.

"Getting divorced is a bummer any time of year," she said. "Over the holidays it's a *mega*bummer. Everywhere I turn, I hear "Have Yourself a Merry Little Christmas," or something equally depressing."

Tanner turned on the gas under a skillet and dobbed in some butter, recalling the first Christmas after Kat's death. He'd left Sophie with Tessa, checked in to a hotel and gone on a bourbon binge.

Not one of his finer moments.

When he'd sobered up, he'd sworn off the bottle and stuck to it.

"Look, Tess," he said gruffly. "Call one of those horse transport outfits and send the hay-burners out here. I've got a barn." Yeah, one that was falling down around his ears, he thought, but he owned a construction company. He could call in the crew early, the one he'd scheduled for Monday, pay them overtime for working the holiday weekend. "This is a big house, so there's plenty of room. And Sophie says the place needs a woman's touch."

Tess was quiet. "Feeling sorry for your kid sister, huh?"

"A little," Tanner said. "You're going through a tough time, and I hate that. But maybe getting away for a while would do you some good. Besides, I could use the help."

She laughed, and though it was a mere echo of the old, rich sound, it was still better than the brave resignation he'd heard in Tessa's voice up till then. "Sophie's still a handful, then."

"Sophie," Tanner said, "is a typhoon, followed by a tidal wave, followed by —"

"You haven't met anybody yet?"

Tanner wasn't going anywhere near that one — not yet, anyway. Sure, he'd gone to bed with one very pretty veterinarian, but they'd both agreed on the no-strings rule. "You never know what might happen," he said, too heartily, hedging.

Another pause, this one thoughtful. "I can't really afford to travel right now, Tanner. Especially not with six horses."

141

The eggs sizzled in the pan. Since he'd forgotten to put in chopped onions — did he even *have* an onion? — he decided he and Sophie would be having scrambled eggs for breakfast, instead of an omelet. "I can make a transfer from my account to yours, on my laptop," he said. "And I'm going to do that, Tess, whether you agree to come out to Arizona or not."

"It's hard being here," Tessa confessed bleakly. That was when he knew she was wavering. "The fight is wearing me out. Lawyers are coming out of the woodwork. I'm not even sure I want this place anymore." A short silence. Tanner knew Tess was grappling with that formidable pride of hers. "I could really bring the horses?"

"Sure," he said. "I'll make the arrangements."

"I'd rather handle that myself," Tessa said. He could tell she was trying not to cry. Once they were off the phone, she'd let the tears come. All by herself in that big Kentucky farmhouse that wasn't a home anymore. "Thanks, Tanner. As brothers go, you're not half-bad."

He chuckled. "Thanks." He was about to offer to line up one of Jack McCall's jets to bring her west, but he decided that would be pushing it. Tessa was nothing if not self-reliant, and she might balk at coming to Stone Creek at all if he didn't let her make at least some of the decisions.

Sophie clattered into the kitchen, wearing yesterday's jeans, funky boots with fake fur around the tops and a heavy cableknit sweater. Her face shone from scrubbing, and she'd pulled her hair back in a ponytail.

"Talk to Hurricane Sophie for a minute, will you?" he asked, to give his sister a chance to collect herself. "I'm about to burn the eggs."

"Aunt Tessa?" Sophie crowed into the phone. "I'm at Dad's new place, and it's way awesome, even if it is a wreck. The wallpaper's peeling in my room, and my ceiling sags . . ."

Tanner rolled his eyes and set about rescuing breakfast.

"*Serious* shopping is required," Sophie went on, after listening to Tess for a few seconds. Or, more properly, waiting for her aunt to shut up so she could talk again. "But first I want to ride Butterpie. Dad's going to let me take her back to school —"

Tanner tuned out the conversation, making toast and a mental grocery list at the same time.

"When will you get here?" Sophie asked excitedly.

143

Tanner tuned back in. He'd forgotten to ask that question while he was on the phone with Tessa.

"You'll get here when you get here," Sophie repeated after a few beats, smiling. "Before Christmas, though, right?" Catching Tanner's eye, Sophie nodded. "Keep us updated . . . I love you, too . . . I'll tell him — bye."

Tanner lobbed partially cold eggs onto plates. "No ETA for Aunt Tessa?" he asked. He set the food on the table and then went to the counter to boot up his laptop. As soon as he'd eaten, he'd pipe some cash into his sister's depleted bank account.

"She loves you." Sophie's eyes danced with anticipation. "She said she's got some stuff to do before she comes to Arizona, but she'll definitely be here before Christmas."

Tanner sat down and ate, but his brain was so busy, he barely tasted the eggs and toast. Which was probably good, since he wasn't the best cook in this or any other solar system. Then again, he wasn't the worst, either.

"You know what I want for Christmas?" Sophie asked, half an hour later as she washed dishes at the old-fashioned sink and Tanner sat at the table, tapping at the keyboard on his laptop. "And don't say,

'Your two front teeth,' either, because that would be a *really* lame joke."

Tanner grinned. "Okay, I won't," he said with mock resignation. "What do you want for Christmas?"

"I want you and me and Aunt Tessa to live here forever," she said. "Like a family. An aunt isn't the same as a mom, but we're all blood, the three of us. It could work."

Tanner's fingers froze in midtap. "Honey," he said quietly, "Aunt Tessa's young. She'll get married again eventually, and have a family of her own, just like you will when you grow up."

"I want to have a family *now*," Sophie said stubbornly. "I've been waiting long enough." With that, she turned back to the sink, rattling the dishes around, and her spine was rigid.

Tanner closed his eyes for a long moment, then forced himself to concentrate on the task at hand — transferring a chunk of money to Tessa's bank account.

He'd think about the mess he was in later.

Olivia might have driven right past Starcross Ranch on her way to town if Ginger hadn't insisted that they stop and look in on Butterpie. In the cold light of a new day, Olivia wasn't eager to face Tanner Quinn.

145

Last night's wanton hussy had given way to *today's* embarrassed Goody Two-shoes.

And there were other things on her mind, too, most notably Ashley's statement on the phone the night before, that she thought she'd found their mother. No matter how Olivia had prodded, her sister had refused to give up any more information.

Olivia had already called the clinic, and she had a light caseload for the day, since another vet was on call. Normally that would have been a relief — she could buy groceries, get her hair trimmed, do some laundry. But she needed to check on Rodney, and Butterpie wasn't out of the woods yet, either. Yes, Sophie was home, so the pony would be ecstatic.

For as long as Tanner allowed his daughter to stay, that is.

For all Olivia knew, he was already making plans to shuttle the poor kid back to boarding school in a black helicopter.

And that thought led full circle back to her mother.

Had Ashley actually found Delia O'Ballivan — the *real* Delia O'Ballivan, not some ringer hoping to cash in on Brad's fame and fortune?

Olivia's feelings on that score were decidedly mixed. She'd dreamed of a reunion

with her lost mother, just as Ashley and
Melissa had, and Brad, too, at least when
he was younger. They'd all been bereft when
Delia left, especially since their father had
died so soon afterward.

If she hadn't been driving, Olivia would
have closed her eyes against that memory.
She'd been there, the tomboy child, always
on horseback, riding with her dad after
some stray cattle, when the lightning struck,
killing both him and his horse instantly.

She'd jumped off her own panicked mount
and run to her dad, kneeling beside him in
the dirt while a warm rain pelted down on
all of them. She'd screamed — and
screamed — and screamed.

Screamed until her throat was raw, until
Big John came racing out into the field in
his old truck.

For a long time she'd thought he'd heard
her cries all the way from the house, the
better part of a mile away. Later, weeks after
the funeral, when the numbness was just
beginning to subside, she'd realized he'd
been passing on the road, and had seen that
bolt of lightning jag down out of the sky.
Seen his own son killed, come running and
stumbling to kneel in the pounding rain,
just as Olivia had, gathering his grown boy

into his strong rancher's arms, and rocking him.

No, Big John had wailed, over and over again, his craggy face awash with tears and rain. *No!*

All these years later Olivia could still hear those cries, and they still tore holes in her heart.

Tears washed her own cheeks.

Ginger, seated on the passenger side of the Suburban as usual, leaned over to nudge Olivia's shoulder.

Olivia sniffled, straightened her shoulders and dashed her face dry with the back of one hand. Her father's death had made the local and regional news, and for a while Olivia had hoped her mother would see the reports, on television or in a newspaper, realize how badly her family needed her and come home.

But Delia *hadn't* come home. Either she'd never learned that her ex-husband, the man to whom she'd borne four children, was dead, or she simply hadn't cared enough to spring for a bus ticket.

Fantasizing about her return had been one thing, though, and knowing it might *actually happen* was another.

She sucked in a deep breath and blew it out hard, making her bangs dance against

148

her forehead.

Maybe Delia, if she *was* Delia, still wouldn't want to come home. That would be a blow to Ashley, starry-eyed optimist that she was. Ashley lived in a Thomas Kinkade sort of world, full of lighted stone cottages and bridges over untroubled waters.

The snow was melting, but the ground was frozen hard, and the Suburban bumped and jostled as Olivia drove up Tanner's driveway. She stopped the rig, intending to stay only a few minutes, and got out. Ginger jumped after her without waiting to use the ramp.

The barn, alas, was empty. Shiloh's and Butterpie's stall doors stood open. Tanner and Sophie must have gone out riding, which should have been a relief — now she would have a little more time before she had to face him — but wasn't. For some reason she didn't want to examine too closely, nervous as she was, she'd been looking forward to seeing Tanner.

She came out of the barn, scanned the fields, saw them far off in the distance, two small figures on horseback. She hesitated only a few moments, then summoned Ginger and headed for the Suburban. She was about to climb behind the wheel when she noticed that the dog had stayed behind.

"You coming?" she called, her voice a little shaky.

"I'll stay here for a while," Ginger answered without turning around. She was gazing off toward Sophie and Tanner.

Olivia swallowed an achy, inexplicable lump. "Don't go chasing after them, okay? Wait on the porch or something."

Ginger didn't offer a reply, or turn around. But she didn't streak off across the field as she had the morning before, either. Short of forcing the animal into the truck, Olivia didn't know what else to do besides leave.

Her first stop was Stone Creek Ranch. As she had at Starcross, she avoided the house and made for the barn. With luck, she wouldn't run into Brad, and have to go into all her concerns about Ashley's mother search.

Luck wasn't with her. Brad O'Ballivan, the world-famous, multi-Grammy-winning singer, was mucking out stalls, the reindeer tagging at his heels like a faithful hound as he worked.

He stopped, leaned on his pitchfork and offered a lopsided grin as Olivia approached, though his eyes were troubled.

"I see Rodney's getting along all right," Olivia said, her voice swelling, strangely thick, in her throat, and nearly cutting off her breath.

Brad gave a solemn nod. Tried for another grin and missed. "I'll have a blue Christmas if Santa comes to reclaim this little guy," he said. "I've gotten attached."

Olivia managed a smile, tried to catch it when it slipped off her mouth by biting her lower lip, and failed. "Why the sad face, cowboy?"

"I was about to ask you the same question — sans the cowboy part."

"Ashley thinks she found Mom," Olivia said.

Brad nodded glumly, set the pitchfork aside, leaning it against the stable wall. Crouched to pet Rodney for a while before steering him back into his stall and shutting the door.

"I guess the time has come to talk about this," Brad said. "Pull up a bale of hay and sit down."

Olivia sat, but it felt more like sinking. Bits of hay poked her through the thighs of her jeans. All the starch, as Big John used to say, had gone out of her knees.

Brad sat across from her, studied her face and said — nothing.

"Where are Meg and Mac?" Olivia asked.

"Mac's with his grandma McKettrick,"

151

Brad answered. "Meg's shopping with Sierra and some of the others."

Olivia nodded. Knotted her hands together in her lap. "Brad, talk to me. Tell me what you know about Mom — because you know *something.* I can tell."

"She's alive," Brad said.

Olivia stared at him, astonished, and angry, too. "And you didn't think the rest of us might be interested in that little tidbit of information?"

"She's a drunk, Livie," Brad told her, holding her gaze steadily. He looked as miserable as Olivia felt. "I tried to help her — she wouldn't be helped. When she calls, I still cut her a check — against my better judgment."

Olivia actually felt the barn sway around her. She had to lean forward and put her head between her knees and tell herself to breathe slowly.

Brad's hand came to rest on her shoulder. She shook it off. *"Don't!"*

"Liv, our mother is not a person you'd want to know," Brad said quietly. "This isn't going to turn out like one of those TV movies, where everybody talks things through and figures out that it's all been one big, tragic misunderstanding. Mom left because she didn't want to be married, and she sure as hell didn't want to raise four kids. And there's no evidence that she's changed, except for the worse."

Olivia lifted her head. The barn stopped spinning like the globe Big John used to keep in his study. What had happened to that globe?

"What's she like?"

"I told you, Liv — she's a drunk."

"She's got to be more than that. The worst drunk in the world is more than just a drunk. . . ."

Brad sighed, intertwined his fingers, let his hands fall between his knees. The look in his eyes made Olivia ache. "She's pretty, in a faded-rose sort of way. Too thin, because she doesn't eat. Her hair's blond, but not shiny and thick like it was when we knew her before. She's — hard, Olivia."

"How long have you been in touch with her?"

"I'm not 'in touch' with her," Brad answered gently, though his tone was gruff. "She called my manager a few years ago, told him she was my mother, and when Phil passed the word on to me, I went to see her. She didn't ask about Dad, or Big John, or any of you. She wanted to —" He stopped, looked away, his head slightly bowed under whatever he was remembering about that pilgrimage.

"Cash in on being Brad O'Ballivan's mother?" Olivia supplied.

"Something like that," Brad replied, meeting Olivia's eyes again, though it obviously wasn't easy. "She's bad news, Liv. But she won't come back to Stone Creek — not even if it means having a ticket to ride the gravy train. She flat out doesn't want anything to do with this place, or with us."

"Why?"

"Damn, Liv. Do you think I know the answer to that any better than you do? This has been harder on you and the twins — I realize that. Girls need a mother. But there were plenty of times when I could have used one, too."

Olivia reached out, touched her brother's arm. He'd had a hard time, especially after their dad was killed. He and Big John had butted heads constantly, mostly because they were so much alike — strong, stubborn, proud to a fault. And they'd been estranged after Brad ran off to Nashville and stayed there.

Oh, Brad had visited a few times over the years. But he'd always left again, over Big John's protests, and then the heart attack came, and it was too late.

"Are you thinking about Big John?" he asked.

It was uncanny, the way he could see into her head sometimes. "Yeah," she said. "His opinion of Delia was even lower than yours. He'd probably have stood at the door with a shotgun if she'd showed her face in Stone Creek."

"The door? He'd have been up at the gate, standing on the cattle guard," Brad answered with a slight shake of his head. "Liv, what are we going to do about Ashley? I think Melissa's levelheaded enough to deal with this. But Ash is in for a shock here. A pretty bad one."

"Is there something else you aren't telling me?"

Brad held up his right hand, as if to give an oath. "I've told you the whole ugly truth, insofar as I know it."

"I'll talk to Ashley," she said.

"Good luck," Brad said.

Olivia started to stand, planning to leave, but Brad stopped her by laying a hand on her shoulder.

"Hold on a second," he told her. "There *is* one more thing I need to say."

Olivia waited, wide-eyed and a little alarmed.

He drew a deep breath, let it out as a

reluctant sigh. "About Tanner Quinn," he began.

Olivia stiffened. Brad could not possibly know what had happened between her and Tanner — could he? He wasn't *that* perceptive.

"What about him?"

"He's a decent guy, Liv," Brad told her. "But —"

"But?"

"Did he tell you about his wife? How she died?"

Olivia shook her head, wondering if Brad was about to say the circumstances had been suspicious, like in one of those reality crime shows on cable TV.

"Her name was Katherine," Brad said. "He called her Kat. He won the bid on a construction job in a place where, let's just say, Americans aren't exactly welcome. It was a dangerous project, but there were millions at stake, so he agreed. One day the two of them went to one of those open-air markets — a souk I think they call it. Tanner stopped to look at something, and Kat either didn't notice or didn't wait for him. When she reached the street . . ." Brad paused, his eyes as haunted as if he'd been there himself. "Somebody strafed the market with some kind of automatic weapon.

156

Snoopy and his decorated doghouse in the cartoon Christmas special she'd watched faithfully since she was three years old. The image cheered her a little.

"Commercial dog," she muttered, though Ashley didn't qualify for the term species-wise, waving to the light crew before pulling away from the curb again.

She ought to see if she could swing a haircut, she thought, cruising the slush-crusty main street of Stone Creek. Every street lamp and every store window was decorated, colored bulbs blinking the requisite bright red and green.

The Christmas-tree man had set up for business down by the supermarket — a new guy this year, she'd heard — and a plump Santa was already holding court in a spiffy-looking black sleigh with holly leaves and berries decorating its graceful lines. Its brass runners gleamed authentically, and eight life-size plastic reindeer had been hitched to the thing with a jingle-bell harness.

Olivia pulled into the lot — before she saw Tanner's red truck parked among other vehicles. She should have noticed it, she thought — it was the only clean one. She shifted into reverse, but it was too late.

Tanner, delectable in jeans and a black leather jacket, caught sight of her and

159

waved. His young daughter, she of the dramatic helicopter arrival, stood beside him, clapping mittened hands together to keep warm as she inspected a tall, lush tree.

Annoyed by her own reticence, Olivia sighed, pulled into one of the few remaining parking spots and shut off the Suburban.

"Hey," Tanner said as she approached, working hard to smile.

Sophie was a very beautiful child — a Christmas angel in ordinary clothes. She probably looked just like her mother, the woman who had died so tragically, in Tanner's arms, no less. The one he'd loved too much to ever forget, according to Brad.

While they were making love the day before, had Tanner been pretending Olivia was Katherine?

Olivia blushed. Amped up her smile.

"Olivia O'Ballivan," Tanner said quietly, his eyes watchful, even a little pensive as he studied her face, "meet my daughter, Sophie."

Sophie turned, smiled and put out a hand. "Hello," she said. "Dad says you're a veterinarian, and you took care of Butterpie. Thank you."

Something melted, in a far and usually inaccessible corner of Olivia's heart. "You're welcome," she answered brightly. "And so is

Butterpie."

"What do you think of this tree?" Sophie asked next, turning to the massive, fragrant blue spruce she'd been examining when Olivia drove in.

Olivia's gaze slid to Tanner's face, sprang away again. "It's — it's lovely," she said.

"Ho! Ho! Ho!" bellowed the hired Santa Claus. Apparently the guy hadn't heard that the line was now considered offensive to women.

"Would you believe this place is run by a man named Kris Kringle?" Sophie said to Olivia, drawing her in somehow, making her feel included, as though they couldn't buy the tree unless she approved of it.

Tanner nudged Sophie's shoulder with a light motion of one elbow. "It's an alias, kid," he said out of the side of his mouth in a pretty respectable imitation of an old-time gangster.

"Duh," Sophie said, but she beamed up at her father, her face aglow with adoration. "And I thought he was *really* Santa Claus."

"Go get Mr. Kringle, so we can wrap this deal up," Tanner told her.

Did he see, Olivia wondered, how much the child loved him? How much she needed him?

Sophie hurried off to find the proprietor.

161

"I take it Sophie will be around for Christmas," Olivia ventured.

"Until New Year's," Tanner said with a nod. "Then she goes straight back to Connecticut. Butterpie's going along — he'll board in a stable near the school until Briarwood's is built — so you won't have to worry about a depressed horse."

Olivia's throat thickened. All her emotions were close to the surface, she supposed because of the holidays and the situation with her mother, which might well morph into a Situation, and the knowledge that all good things seemed to be temporary.

"I'll miss Butterpie," she managed, shoving her cold hands into the pockets of her old down vest. It was silly to draw comparisons between her own issues and Sophie's, but she couldn't seem to help it. She was entangled.

"I'll miss Sophie," Tanner said.

Olivia wanted to beat at his chest with her fists, which just went to prove she needed therapy. *She needs you!* she wanted to scream. *Don't you see that you're all she has?*

Patently none of her business. She pretended an interest in a small potted tree nearby, a Charlie Brown-ish one that suited her mood. Right then and there she decided to buy it, take it home and toss some lights onto it.

It was an act of mercy.

"Olivia —" Tanner began, and his tone boded something serious, but before he could get the rest of the sentence out of his mouth, Sophie was back with Kris Kringle.

Olivia very nearly didn't believe what she was seeing. The man wore ordinary clothes — quilted snow pants, a heavy plaid flannel shirt, a blue down vest and a Fargo hat with earflaps. But he had a full white beard and kind — okay, *twinkly* — blue eyes. Round red cheeks, and a bow of a mouth.

"A fine choice indeed," he told Olivia, noting her proximity to the pathetic little tree no one else was likely to buy. Only the thought of it, sitting forgotten on the lot when Christmas arrived, amid a carpet of dried-out pine needles, kept her from changing her mind. "I could tie on some branches for you with twine. Thicken it up a little."

Olivia shook her head, rummaged in her pocket for money, being very careful not to look at Tanner and wondering why she felt the need to do that. "It's fine the way it is. How much?"

Kringle named a figure, and Olivia forked over the funds. She felt stupid, being so protective of a tree, and she didn't even own any decorations, but Charlie Brown was going home with her anyway. They'd just have to make the best of things.

"Dad told me you found a real reindeer," Sophie said to Olivia when she would have grabbed her tree, said goodbye and made a hasty retreat.

This drew Kris Kringle's attention, Olivia noted out of the corner of her eye. He perked right up, listening intently. Zeroing in. If he thought he was going to use that poor little reindeer to attract customers, he had another think coming.

Sure enough, he said, "I just happen to be missing a reindeer."

Olivia didn't believe him, and even though she knew that was because she didn't *want* to believe him, her radar was up and her antennae were beeping. "Is that so?" she asked somewhat stiffly, while Tanner and Sophie looked on with heightened interest. "How did you happen to misplace this reindeer, Mr. — ?"

"Kringle," the old man insisted with a smile in his eyes. "We did a personal appearance at a birthday party, and he just wandered off."

"I see," Olivia said. "Didn't you look for him?"

164

"Oh, yes," Kringle replied, looking like a right jolly old elf and all that. "No tracks to be found. We hunted and hunted. Is Rodney all right?"

Olivia's mouth fell open. Kringle *must* be the reindeer's rightful owner if he knew his name. It would be too much of a coincidence otherwise. "He's — he's fine," she said.

Kringle smiled warmly. "The other seven have been *very* worried, and so have I, although I've had an idea all along that Rodney was on a mission of some kind."

Olivia swallowed. She'd wanted to find Rodney's rightful owner so he could go home. So why did she feel so dejected?

"The other seven what?" Tanner asked with a dry note in his voice.

"Why, the other seven reindeer, of course," Kringle answered merrily after tossing a conspiratorial glance Sophie's way. "If Rodney is safe and well taken care of, though, we won't fret about him. Not until Christmas Eve, anyway. We'll need him back by then for sure."

If Olivia had had a trowel handy, she would have handed it to the guy, so he could lay it on thicker. He really knew how to tap in to Christmas, that was for sure.

"I thought Santa's reindeer had names

like Prancer and Dancer," Sophie said, sounding serious.

Tanner, meanwhile, got out his wallet to pay for the big spruce.

"Well, they do," Kringle said, still in Santa mode. "But they're getting older, and Donner's developed a touch of arthritis. So I brought Rodney up out of the ranks, since he showed so much promise, especially at flying. He's only been on trial runs so far, but this Christmas Eve he's on the flight manifest for the whole western region."

Tanner and Olivia exchanged looks.

"You don't need Rodney back until Christmas Eve?" Olivia asked. An owner was an owner, crazy or not. She took one of her dog-eared business cards out of her vest pocket, wrote Brad's private number on the back with a pen Tanner provided and handed it to Kringle. "He's at Stone Creek Ranch."

"I'll pick him up after I close the lot on the twenty-fourth," Kringle said, still twinkling, and even going so far as to tap a finger to the side of his nose. If there had been a chimney handy, he probably would have rocketed right up it. He examined the card, nodded to himself and tucked it away. "Around six o'clock," he added. "Even the last-minute Louies will have cleared out by then."

"Right," Olivia murmured, wondering if she'd made a mistake telling him where to find Rodney.

"Let me load up that tree for you," Tanner said, hoisting Charlie Brown by his skinny, crooked trunk before Olivia could get a hold on it. Brown needles rained to the pavement.

Sophie tagged along with Tanner and Olivia while Kringle carried the big spruce to Tanner's pickup truck. Branches of the lush tree rustled, and the evergreen scent intensified.

A few fat flakes of snow wafted down.

Olivia felt like a figure in a festive snow globe. Man, woman and child, with Christmas tree. Which was silly.

"My tree weighs all of three pounds," she pointed out to Tanner under her breath. "Aren't you supposed to be working on the new shelter?"

"More like thirty, with this pot." Tanner grinned and held the little tree out of her reach. "Nothing much gets done on a holiday weekend," he added, as if it was some big news flash or something. "Shouldn't you be helping a cow give birth?"

167

"Cows don't commonly give birth at this time of year," Olivia pointed out. "It's a springtime sort of thing."

"Yeah, Dad," Sophie interjected, rolling her eyes. "Yeesh."

Olivia had to laugh. "Yeah," she said, opening the rear doors of the Suburban to receive Charlie Brown. *"Yeesh."*

"How about joining Sophie and me for supper tonight?" Tanner asked, blocking the way when she would have closed the doors again.

"We live in a dump," Sophie said philosophically. "But it's home."

Olivia felt another pang at the word *home.* The rental she lived in definitely didn't qualify, and though she had a history at Stone Creek Ranch, it belonged to Brad and Meg and Mac now, which was as it should be. "Well . . ."

"Please?" Sophie asked, suddenly earnest.

Tanner grinned, waited. The kid was virtually irresistible, and nobody knew that better than he did.

"Okay," Olivia said. For Sophie's sake and not — not *at all* — because she wanted to get in any deeper with Tanner Quinn than she already was.

"Six o'clock?" Tanner asked.

"Six o'clock," Olivia confirmed, casting

another glance at Kris Kringle, now busy instructing the hired Santa Claus on how to hold the sleigh reins. She'd call Wyatt Terp, the marshal over in Indian Rock, the county seat, she decided, and get him to run a background check on this dude, just in case he had a rap sheet or the men in white coats were looking for him.

Tanner and Sophie said their goodbyes and left, and Olivia sat in the driver's seat of her Suburban for a few moments, working up the courage to call Wyatt. The only name she could give him was Kris Kringle, and *that* was bound to liven up an otherwise dull day in the cop shop.

"You mean there really *is* a Kris Kringle?" she asked ten minutes later, her cell phone pressed to one ear as she pulled into the lot at the hardware store to buy lights and tinsel for Charlie Brown.

"You'd be surprised how many there are," Wyatt said drolly.

"So you have something on him, then? You're sure it's the same guy?"

"Kristopher Kringle, it says here. Christmas-tree farmer with a place up near Flagstaff. Only one traffic violation — he was caught driving a horse-drawn sleigh on the freeway two winters ago."

Olivia shut off the Suburban, eyes popping. The painted sign on the weathered brick side of the hardware store read, in time-faded letters, "Smoke Caliber Cigarettes. They're Good for You!"

"Nothing like, say, animal cruelty?"

"Nope," Wyatt said. Olivia could hear some yukking going on in the background. Either the cops were celebrating early or the marshal had the phone on "speaker." "Santa's clean, Doc."

Olivia sighed. She was relieved, of course, to learn that Kringle was neither an escaped maniac nor a criminal, but on some level, she realized, she'd been hoping *not* to find Rodney's owner.

How crazy was that?

She got out of the car, after promising Charlie Brown she'd be back soon, and went inside to shop for a tree wardrobe. She bought two strands of old-fashioned bubbling lights, a box of shiny glass balls in a mixture of red, gold and silver, and some tinsel.

Ho, ho, ho, she thought, stashing her purchases in the back of the rig, next to Charlie. *Deck the halls.*

Even though they had a million things to do, Sophie insisted on stopping at Stone Creek Middle School when they drove past it. It was a small brick building, and the reader board in front read "Closed for Thanksgiving Vacation! See You Monday!"

The whole town, Tanner thought, feeling grumbly, was relentlessly cheerful. And what was up with that Kris Kringle yahoo, back at the tree lot, claiming he had seven reindeer at home, waiting to lift off on Christmas Eve?

Sophie cupped her hands and peered through the plate-glass door at the front of the school, her breath fogging it up. "Wow," she said. "The computer room at Briarwood is bigger than this whole place."

"Can we go now, Soph? We still need to pick up lights and ornaments and some things for you to wear, not to mention groceries."

Sophie turned and made a face at him. "Bah-humbug," she said. "Why are you so crabby all of a sudden?" She paused to waggle her eyebrows. "You looked real happy when Olivia was around."

"That guy at the tree lot . . ."

"What?" Sophie said, skipping back down the snowy steps to the walk. "You think he's a serial killer or something, just because he claims to be Santa?"

"Where do you get these things?" Tanner asked.

"He's delusional, that's all," said the doctor's daughter. "And probably harmless."

"Probably," Tanner agreed. He knew then what was troubling him — Olivia clearly didn't want to surrender custody of the reindeer until she knew "Kris Kringle" was all right. And he cared, more than he liked, what Olivia wanted and didn't want.

"Danger lurks everywhere!" Sophie teased, making mitten claws with her hands in an attempt to look scary. "You just can't be *too careful!*"

"Cut it out, goofball," Tanner said, chuckling in spite of himself as they both got back in the truck. "You don't know anything about the world. If you did, you wouldn't have run away from the field trip and tried to board an iron horse headed west."

"Are we going to talk about *that* again?" Sophie fastened her seat belt with exaggerated care. "I'm a proactive person, Dad. Don't you want me to be *proactive?*"

Tanner didn't answer. Whatever he said would be wrong.

"That Santa shouldn't be saying 'ho, ho, ho,' " Sophie informed him as they pulled away from the curb. Next stop, the ranch, to drop off the tree, then on to a mall he'd checked on MapQuest, outside Flagstaff.

"It isn't politically correct."

"Ask me what I think of political correctness," Tanner retorted.

"Why would I do that when I already know?" Sophie responded cheerfully. "At Briarwood we call Valentine's Day 'Special Relationship Day' now."

"What's next? 'Significant Parental Figure Day' for Father's and Mother's Day?"

Sophie laughed, her cheeks bright with cold and excitement. "It does sound kind of silly, doesn't it?"

"Big-time," Tanner said. He couldn't even tell a woman on his executive staff that her hair looked nice without risking a sexual-harassment suit. Where would it all end?

At home, Tanner unloaded the tree and set it on the front porch so the branches could settle, while Sophie went out to the barn to eyeball the horses. In looks she resembled Kat, but she sure took after Tessa when it came to hay-burners.

"That dog is still here," she reported when she came back. "The one that was waiting on the porch when we got back from riding this morning. Shouldn't we take her home or something?"

"Ginger lives next door, with Olivia," Tanner reminded Sophie. "If she wants to go home, she can get there on her own."

"I hope she isn't depressed, like Butterpie was," Sophie fretted.

Tanner grinned, gave her ponytail a light tug. "She and Butterpie are buddies," he said, recalling finding the dog in the pony's stall. "Olivia will take her home after supper tonight, most likely."

"You like Olivia, don't you?" Sophie asked, with a touch of slyness, as she climbed back into the truck.

Tanner got behind the wheel, started the engine. Olivia was right. The rig was too clean — it had stood out like the proverbial sore thumb back in town, at the tree lot. Maybe he could find a creek to run it through or something. With the ground frozen hard, it wouldn't be easy to come up with mud.

So where were the other guys getting all that macho dirt streaking their rigs and clogging their grilles?

"Of course I like her," he said. "She's a friend."

"She's pretty."

"I'll grant you that one, shorty. She's very pretty."

"You could marry her."

Tanner, in the process of turning the truck around, stopped it instead. "Don't go there, Soph. Olivia's a hometown girl, with a family and a veterinary practice. I'll be moving on to a new place after Stone Creek. And neither one of us is looking for a serious relationship."

Sophie sighed, and her shoulders sloped as though the weight of the world had just been laid on them. "I almost wish that Kris Kringle guy really was Santa Claus," she said. "Then I could tell him I want a mom for Christmas."

Tanner knew he was being played, but his eyes burned and his throat tightened just the same. No accounting for visceral reactions. "That was pretty underhanded, Soph," he said. "It was blatant manipulation. And guilt isn't going to work with me. You should know that by now."

Sophie folded her arms and sulked. Only twelve and already she'd mastered the you're-too-stupid-to-live look teenage girls were so good at. Tessa had been world champ, but clearly the torch had been passed. "What*ever.*"

"I know you'd like to have a mother, Sophie."

"You know, but you don't care."

"I *do* care."

A tear slid down Sophie's left cheek, and Tanner knew it wasn't orchestrated to win his sympathy, because she turned her head quickly, so he wouldn't see.

"I do care, Sophie," he repeated.

She merely nodded. Gave a sniffle that tore at his insides.

Maybe someday she'd understand that he was only trying to protect her. Maybe she wouldn't.

He wondered if he could deal with the latter possibility. Suppose, even as a grown woman, Sophie still resented him?

Well, he thought grimly, this wasn't *about* him. It was about keeping Sophie safe, whether she liked it or not.

He took the turnoff for Flagstaff, bypassing Stone Creek completely. Sophie was female. Shopping would make her feel better, and if that didn't work, there was still the Christmas tree to set up, and Olivia coming over for supper.

They'd get through this, he and Sophie.

"The time's going to go by really fast," Sophie lamented, breaking the difficult silence and still not looking at him. "Before I know it, I'll be right back at Briarwood. Square one."

Tanner waited a beat to answer, so he wouldn't snap at the kid. God knew, being twelve years old in this day and age couldn't be easy, what with all the drugs and the underground Web sites and the movement to rename *Valentine's Day,* for God's sake. No, it would be difficult with two ordinary parents and a mortgaged house, and Sophie didn't have two parents.

She didn't even have *one,* really.

"Everything's going to be all right, Soph," he said. Was he trying to convince her, or himself? Both, probably.

"I could live with Aunt Tessa on Starcross — couldn't I? And go to Stone Creek Middle School, like a regular kid?"

Tanner nearly had to pull over to the side of the road. Instead, he clamped his jaw down tight and concentrated harder on navigating the slick high-country road curving ever upward into the timbered area around Flagstaff.

He should have seen this coming, after the way Sophie had made him stop at the school in town so she could look in the windows, but the kid had a gift for blindsiding him.

"Aunt Tessa," he said evenly, "is only visiting for the holidays."

"She's bringing her horses."

"Okay, a few months at most. Can we not talk about this for a little while, Soph? Because it's a fast track to nowhere."

That was when she brought out the big guns. "They have drugs at Briarwood, you know," she said with a combination of defiance and bravado. "It's not an ivory tower, no matter *how* good the security is."

That time he *did* pull over, with a screech of tires and a lot of flying slush. *"What?"* he rasped.

"Meth," Sophie said. "Ice. That's —"

"I *know* what ice is," Tanner snapped. "So help me God, Sophie, if you're messing with me —"

"It's true, Dad."

He believed her. That was the worst thing of all. His stomach rolled, and for a moment he thought he might have to shove open the door and get sick, right then and there.

"It's a pervasive problem," Sophie said, sounding like a venerable news commentator instead of a preadolescent girl.

"Has anyone offered you drugs? Have you taken any?" He kept his hand on the door handle, just in case.

"I'm not stupid, Dad," she answered. "Drugs are for losers, people who can't cope unless their brains have been chemically altered."

"Would you talk like a twelve-year-old for a few minutes? Just to humor me?"

"I don't take drugs, Dad," Sophie reiterated quietly.

"How are they getting in? The drugs, I mean?"

"Kids bring them from home. I think they mostly steal them from their parents."

Tanner laid his forehead on the steering wheel and drew slow, deep breaths. *From their parents.* In his mind, he started drawing up blueprints for an ivory tower. Not that he'd use ivory, even if he could get it from a legitimate supplier.

Sophie touched his arm. "Dad, I'm trying to make a point here. Are you okay? Because you look kind of . . . gray. You're not having a heart attack or anything, are you?"

"Not the kind you're thinking of," Tanner said, straightening. Pulling himself together. He was a father. He needed to act like one.

When he was sure he wasn't a menace to Sophie, himself and the general driving public, he pulled back out onto the highway. Sophie fiddled with the radio until she found a station she liked, and a rap beat filled the truck cab.

Tanner adjusted the dial. Brad O'Ballivan's voice poured out of the speakers. "Have Yourself a Merry Little Christmas."

It figured. Tessa was practically being stalked by the song, according to her, and now he probably would be, too.

"Is that the guy who hired you to build

179

the animal shelter?" Sophie asked.

Beyond relieved at the change of subject, Tanner said, "Yes."

"He has a nice voice."

"That's the word on the street."

"Even if the song *is* kind of hokey."

Tanner laughed. "I'll tell him you said so."

After that they talked about ordinary things — not drugs at Briarwood, not Sophie's longing for a mother, destined to be unrequited, not weird Kris Kringle, the reindeer man. No, they discussed a new saddle for Butterpie, and what to get Tessa for Christmas, and the pros and cons of nuking a package of frozen lasagna for supper.

Reaching the mall, Tanner parked the truck and the two of them waded in. They bought ornaments and lights and tinsel. They cleaned out the "young juniors" department in an upscale store, and chose a yellow cashmere sweater for Tessa's gift. They had a late lunch in the food court, watching as the early shoppers rushed by with their treasures.

On the way out of town they stopped at a Western supply store for the new saddle, and after that, a supermarket, where they filled two carts. When they left the store, Tanner almost tripped over a kid in ragged jeans, a T-shirt and a thin jacket, trying to give away squirmy puppies from a big box. The words "Good Xmas Presents" had been scrawled on the side in black marker.

Tanner lengthened his stride, making the shopping cart wheels rattle.

Sophie stopped her cart.

"Oh, they're so cute," she said.

"Only two left," the kid pointed out unnecessarily. There were holes in the toes of his sneakers. Had he dressed for the part?

"Sophie," Tanner said in warning.

But she'd picked up one of the puppies — a little golden-brown one of indeterminate breed, with floppy ears and big, hopeful eyes. Then the other, a black-and-white version of the dog Tanner remembered from his first-grade reader.

"Dad," she whispered, drawing up close to his side, the full cart she'd been pushing left behind by the boy and the box, to show him the puppies. "Look at that kid. He probably needs the money, and who knows what might happen to these poor little things if they don't get sold?"

Tanner couldn't bring himself to say the obvious — that Sophie would be leaving for a new school in a few weeks, since Briarwood was definitely out of the question now that he knew about the drugs. He'd just have to buy the dogs and hope that Olivia would be able to find them good homes when the time came.

At the moment, turning Sophie down wasn't an option, even if it was the right thing to do. He'd had to say no to one too many things already.

So Tanner gave the boy a ridiculous amount of money for the puppies, and Sophie scared them half to death with a squeal of delight, and they loaded up the grub and the dogs and headed back to Starcross Ranch.

CHAPTER EIGHT

Olivia hadn't been able to track Ashley down, even after hunting all over town, and no emergency veterinary calls came in, either. She had her hair cut at the Curly-Q, bought some groceries and cleaning supplies at the supermarket, then she and Charlie Brown went home.

Ginger was waiting on the back porch when she arrived, balls of snow clinging to her legs and haunches from the walk across the very white field between Olivia's place and Tanner's.

"It's about time you got here," the dog said, rising off her nest of blankets next to the drier.

Freezing, Olivia hustled through the kitchen door and set Charlie Brown on the table, root-bound in his bulky plastic pot. "You're the one who insisted on staying at Starcross," she said before going back out for the bags from the hardware store and supermarket.

A pool of melted snow surrounded Ginger when Olivia finished carrying everything inside. After setting the last of the bags on the counter, she threw an old towel into the drier to warm it up and adjusted the thermostat for the temperamental old furnace. She started a pot of coffee — darn, she should have picked up a new brewing apparatus at the hardware store — and filled Ginger's kibble bowl.

While the dog ate and the coffee brewed, Olivia fished the towel out of the drier and knelt on the scuffed and peeling linoleum floor to give Ginger a rubdown.

"Were they out of good Christmas trees?" Ginger asked, eyeing Charlie Brown, whose sparse branches seemed to droop a little at the insult.

"Be nice," Olivia whispered. "You'll hurt his feelings."

"I suppose I should be happy that you're decorating this year," Ginger answered, giving Olivia's face an affectionate lick as thanks for the warm towel. *"Since you're so Christmas-challenged and all."*

Olivia stood, chuckling. "I saw these stick-on reindeer antlers for dogs at the hardware store," she said. "They have jingle bells and they light up. Treat me right or I'll

184

buy you a pair, take your picture and post it on the Internet."

Ginger sighed. She hated costumes.

A glance at the clock told Olivia she had an hour before she was due at Starcross for supper. After her shower, she decided, she'd dig through her closet and bureau drawers again, and find something presentable to wear, so Sophie wouldn't think she was a rube.

Ginger padded after her, jumped up onto her unmade bed and curled up in the middle. Olivia laid out clean underwear, her second-best pair of jeans and a red sweatshirt from two years ago, when Ashley had been on a fabric-painting kick. It had a cutesy snowman on the front, with light-up eyes, though the battery was long dead.

Toweling off after her shower and pulling on her clothes quickly, since even with the thermostat up, the house was drafty, Olivia told Ginger about the invitation to Starcross.

"I'll stay here," Ginger said. *"Reinforcements have arrived."*

"What kind of reinforcements?" Olivia asked, peering at Ginger through the neck hole as she tugged the sweatshirt on over her head.

"You'll see," Ginger answered, her eyes

already at half-mast as she drifted toward sleep. *"Take your kit with you."*

"Is Butterpie sick?" Olivia asked, alarmed.

"No," came the canine reply. *"I would have told you right away if she was. But you'll need the kit."*

"Okay," Olivia said.

Ginger's snore covered an octave, somewhere in the alto range.

Olivia wasn't musical.

At six o'clock, straight up, she drove up in front of the ranch house at Starcross. Colored lights glowed through the big picture window, a cheering sight in the snow-flecked twilight.

Bringing her medical kit as far as the porch, Olivia set it down and knocked.

Sophie opened the door, her small face as bright as the tree lights. The scents of piney sap and something savory cooking or cooling added to the ambience.

"Wait till you *see* what we got at the supermarket!" Sophie whooped, half dragging Olivia over the threshold.

Tanner stood framed in the entrance to the living room, one shoulder braced against the woodwork. He wore a blue Henley shirt, with a band around the neck instead of a collar, open at the throat, and jeans that looked as though they'd seen some decent wear. "Yeah," he drawled with an almost imperceptible roll of his eyes, "wait till you see."

A puppy bark sounded from behind him.

"You didn't," Olivia said, secretly thrilled.

"There are *two* of them!" Sophie exulted as the pair gamboled around Tanner to squirm and yip at Olivia's feet.

She crouched immediately, laughing and ruffling small, warm ears. So *this* was the reason Ginger had wanted her to bring the kit. These were mongrels, not purebreds, up to date on their vaccinations before they left the kennel, and they'd need their shots.

"I named them Snidely and Whiplash," Sophie said. "After the villain in *The Dudley Do-Right Show.*"

"I suggested Going and Gone," Tanner interjected humorously, "but the kid wouldn't go for it."

"Which is which?" Olivia asked Sophie, ignoring Tanner's remark. Her heart was beating fast — did this mean he was thinking of staying on at Starcross after the shelter was finished?

"That's Snidely," Sophie said, pointing to the puppy with gold fur. They looked like some kind of collie-shepherd-retriever mix. "The spotted one is Whiplash."

187

"Let's just have a quick look at them," Olivia suggested. "My kit is on the porch. Would you get it for me, please?"

Sophie rushed to comply.

"Going and Gone?" Olivia asked very softly, watching Tanner.

Now that she'd shifted, she could see the blue spruce behind him, in front of the snow-laced picture window.

But Sophie was back before he could answer.

"Later," he mouthed, and his eyes looked so serious that some of the spontaneous Christmas magic drifted to the floor like tired fairy dust.

Olivia examined the puppies, pronounced them healthy and gave them each their first round of shots. They were "box" puppies, giveaways, and that invariably meant they'd had no veterinary care at all.

"Does that hurt them?" Sophie asked, her blue eyes wide as she watched Olivia inject serum into the bunched-up scruffs of their necks with a very small needle. They'd all gathered in the living room, near the fragrant tree and the fire dancing on the hearth, Olivia employing the couch as an examining table.

"No," she said gently, putting away her doctor gear. "The injections will prevent distemper and parvo, among other things. The diseases *would* hurt, and these girls will need to be spayed as soon as they're a little older."

Sophie nodded solemnly. "They wet on the floor," she said, "but I promised Dad I'd clean up after them myself."

"Good girl," Olivia said. "If you take them outside every couple of hours, they'll get the idea." Her gaze was drawn to Tanner, but she resisted. *Going and Gone?* The names didn't bode well. Had he actually brought these puppies home intending to get rid of them as soon as Sophie went back to school?

No, she thought. *He couldn't have. He couldn't be that cold.*

There was lasagna for supper, and salad. Sophie talked the whole time they were eating, fairly bouncing in her chair while the puppies tumbled and played under the table, convinced they had a home.

Even though she was hungry, Olivia couldn't eat much.

When the meal was over, Sophie and Olivia put on coats and went out to the barn to see Butterpie and Shiloh while Tanner, strangely quiet, stayed behind to clean up the kitchen.

"We bought a new saddle for Butterpie,"

Sophie said excitedly as they entered the hay-scented warmth of the barn. "And Dad's having all the stalls fixed up so Aunt Tessa's horses will be comfortable here."

"Aunt Tessa?" Olivia asked, admiring the saddle. She'd had one much like it as a young girl; Big John had bought it for her thirteenth birthday, probably secondhand and at considerable sacrifice to the budget.

Now, she thought sadly, she didn't even own a horse.

"Tessa's my dad's sister. She has a whole bunch of horses, and she's getting a divorce, so Dad sent her money to come out here to Arizona." Sophie drew a breath and rushed on. "Maybe you saw her on TV. She starred in *California Women* for years — and a whole bunch of shows before that."

Olivia remembered the series, though she didn't watch much television. Curiously, her viewing was mostly limited to the holidays — she always tried to catch *It's a Wonderful Life, The Bishop's Wife* and, of course, *A Charlie Brown Christmas.*

"I think I've seen it once or twice," she said, but she couldn't place Tessa's character.

Sophie sagged a little as she opened Butterpie's stall. "I think Dad's going to ask Aunt Tessa to stay here and look after Starcross Ranch and Shiloh and the puppies after he leaves," she said.

"Oh," Olivia said, deflated but keeping up a game face for Sophie's sake.

Butterpie looked fit, and she was eating again.

"I'm still hoping he'll change his mind and let me stay here," Sophie confided quietly. "My education shouldn't be interrupted — at least we agree on that much — so I get to go to Stone Creek Middle School, starting Monday, until they let out for Christmas vacation."

Olivia didn't know what to say. She had opinions about boarding schools and adopting puppies he didn't intend to raise, that was for sure, but sharing them with Sophie would be over the line. Satisfied that Butterpie was doing well, she let herself into Shiloh's stall to stroke his long side.

He nuzzled her affectionately.

And her cell phone rang.

Here it was. The sick-cow call Olivia had been expecting all day.

But the number on the caller ID panel was Melissa's private line at the law office. What was she doing working this late, and on a holiday weekend, too?

"Mel? What's up?"

"It's Ashley," Melissa said quietly. "She

just called me from some Podunk town in Tennessee. She caught the shuttle to the airport early this morning, evidently, and flew out of Phoenix without telling any of us."

"Tennessee?" Olivia echoed, momentarily confused. Or was she simply trying to deny what she already knew, deep down?

"I guess Mom's living there now," Melissa said.

Sophie stepped out of Butterpie's stall just as Olivia stepped out of Shiloh's, her face full of concern. They turned their backs on each other to work the latches, securing both horses for the night.

"Oh, my God," Olivia said.

"She's a wreck," Melissa went on, sounding as numb as Olivia felt. "Ashley, I mean. Things turned out badly — so badly that Brad's chartering a jet to go back there and pick up the pieces."

Sophie caught hold of Olivia's arm, steered her to a bale of hay and urged her to sit down.

She sat, gratefully. Standing up any longer would have been impossible, with her knees shaking the way they were.

"Should I go get my dad?" Sophie asked.

Olivia shook her head, then closed her eyes. "What happened, Mel? What did Ashley say on the phone?"

"She just said she should have listened to you and Brad. She was crying so hard, I could hardly understand her. She told me where she was staying and I called Brad as soon as we hung up."

Ashley. The innocent one, the one who believed in happy endings. She'd just run up against an ugly reality, and Olivia was miles away, unable to help her. "I'm going to call Brad and tell him I want to go, too," she said, about to hang up.

"I tried that," Melissa answered immediately. "He said he wanted to handle this alone. My guess is he's already on his way to Flagstaff to board the jet."

Olivia fought back tears of frustration, fury and resignation. "When did Ashley call?" she asked, fighting for composure. Sophie was already plenty worried — the look on her face proved that — and it wouldn't do to fall apart in front of a child.

"About half an hour ago. I called Brad right away, and we were on the phone for a long time. As soon as we hung up, I called you."

"Thanks," Olivia said woodenly.

"Are you all right?" Melissa asked.

"No," Olivia replied. "Are you?"

"No," Melissa admitted. "And I won't be

until the twin-unit is back home in Stone Creek, where she belongs. I know you want to call Brad and beat your head against a brick wall trying to get him to let you go to Tennessee with him, so I'll let you go."

"Go home," Olivia told her kid sister. "It's a holiday weekend and you shouldn't be working."

Melissa's chuckle sounded more like a sob. Olivia was terrified, so Melissa, what with the twin bond and all, had to be ready to dissolve. "Like *you* have any room to talk," she said. "Can I come out to your place, Liv, and spend the night with you and Ginger?"

"Meet you there," Olivia said, following up with a goodbye. She speed-dialed Brad in the next moment.

"No," he said instead of the customary hello.

"Where are you?"

"Almost to Flagstaff. The jet's waiting. When I know anything, I'll call you."

Clearly, asking him to come back for her, or wait till she could get to the airport, would, as her sister had predicted, be a waste of breath. Besides, Melissa needed her, or she wouldn't have asked to spend the night.

"Okay," Olivia said. A few moments later

she shut her cell phone.

Sophie stood watching her. "Did something bad happen?"

Olivia stood. Her knees were back in working order, then. That was something. "It's a family thing," she said. "Nothing you need to worry about. I have to go home right away, though."

Sophie nodded sagely. "Shall I go get your doctor bag?" she asked. "I'll explain to Dad and everything."

"Thanks," Olivia said, heading for the Suburban.

Sophie raced for the house, but it was Tanner who brought the medical kit out to her.

"Anything I can do?" he asked, handing it through the open window of the Suburban.

Olivia shook her head, not trusting herself to speak.

To her utter surprise, Tanner leaned in, cupped his hand at the back of her head and planted a gentle but electrifying kiss on her mouth. Then he stepped away, and she put the Suburban into gear and drove out.

Tanner stood in the cold, watching Olivia's taillights disappear in the thickening snowfall.

The shimmering colors on the Christmas tree in the front room seemed to mock him through the steam-fogged glass. Whatever Olivia's problem was, he probably couldn't make it right. It was a "family thing," according to Sophie's breathless report, and he wasn't family.

He shoved his hands into his hip pockets — he hadn't bothered with a coat — and thought about, of all things, the puppies. There was no way he could ask Olivia to find them homes after he moved on. Tessa might or might not be willing to stay on at Stone Creek and look after Snidely and Whiplash.

He'd dug himself a big hole, with Sophie *and* with Olivia, and getting out was going to take some doing. Fast-talking wouldn't pack it.

Inside the house, Sophie was making a bed for the puppies in a cardboard box fluffed up with an old blanket.

"Did somebody die?" she asked when Tanner entered the living room.

The question poleaxed him. Sophie had lost her mother when she was seven years old. Did every crisis prompt her to expect a funeral?

"I don't think so, honey," he said gruffly. He should have hugged her, but he couldn't move. He just stood there, like a fool, in the middle of the living room.

Sophie looked at the Christmas tree. "Maybe we could finish decorating tomorrow," she said. "I don't feel much like it now."

"Me, either," Tanner admitted. "Let's take the puppies outside before you bed them down."

Sophie nodded, and they put on their coats and each took a puppy.

The dogs squatted obediently in the thickening snow.

"I like Olivia," Sophie said.

"I do, too," Tanner replied. *Maybe a little too much.*

"It was fun having her here to eat supper with us."

Tanner nodded, draped an arm around Sophie's small shoulders. She felt so little, so insubstantial, inside her bulky nylon jacket.

"I showed her my new saddle."

"It's a nice piece of gear."

The puppies were finished. Tanner scooped one up, and Sophie collected the other. They plodded toward the house, with its half-decorated Christmas tree, peeling wallpaper and outdated plumbing fixtures.

Flipping *this* house, Tanner thought ruefully, was going to be a job.

Once Sophie and the dogs were settled upstairs, in the room she'd declared to be hers, Tanner unplugged the tree lights and wandered into the kitchen to log on at his laptop. He had some supply invoices to look over, fortunately, and that would keep his mind occupied. Keep him from worrying about what had happened in Olivia's family to knock her off balance like that.

He could call Brad and ask, of course, but he wasn't going to do that. It would be an intrusion.

So he poured himself a cup of lukewarm coffee, drew up a chair at the table and opened his laptop.

The invoices were there, all right. But they might as well have been written in Sanskrit, for all the sense he could make of them.

After half an hour he gave up.

It was too early to go to sleep, so he snapped on the one TV set in the house, a little portable in the living room, and flipped through channels until he found a weather report.

Snow, snow and more snow.

He sighed and changed channels again, settled on a holiday rerun of *Everybody Loves Raymond.* Here, at least, was a family even more dysfunctional than his own.

In a perverse sort of way, it cheered him up.

Melissa arrived with an overnight case only twenty minutes after Olivia got home. Her blue eyes were red rimmed from crying.

Of all the O'Ballivan siblings, Melissa was the least emotional. But she stood in Olivia's kitchen, her shoulders stooped and dusted with snowflakes, and choked up when she tried to speak.

Olivia immediately took her younger sister into her arms. "It's okay," she said. "Everything will work out, you'll see."

Melissa nodded, sniffled and pulled away. "God," she said, trying to make a joke, "this place is *such* a dive."

"It'll do until I can move in above the new shelter," Olivia said, pointing toward the nearby hall. "The guest room is ready. Put your stuff away and we'll talk."

Melissa had spotted Charlie Brown, still standing in his nondescript pot in the center of the kitchen table. "You bought a Christmas tree?" she marveled.

Olivia set her hands on her hips. "Why is that such a surprise to everybody?" she asked, realizing only when the words were out of her mouth that *Ginger* had offered the only other comment on the purchase.

Melissa sighed and shook her head. Ginger escorted her to the spare room, and back. Melissa had shed her coat, and she was pushing up the sleeves of her white sweater as she reentered the kitchen.

"Let's get the poor thing decorated," she said.

"Good idea," Olivia agreed.

The tree was fairly heavy, between the root system and the pot, and Melissa helped her lug it into the living room.

Olivia pushed an end table in front of the window, after moving a lamp, and Charlie was hoisted to eye level.

"This is sort of — cheerful," Melissa said, probably being kind, though whether she felt sorry for Olivia or the tree was anybody's guess.

Olivia pulled the bubble lights and ornaments from the hardware-store bags. "Maybe I should make popcorn or something."

"That," Melissa teased after another sniffle, "would constitute *cooking.* And you promised you wouldn't try that at home."

Olivia laughed. "I'm glad you're here, Mel."

"Me, too," Melissa said. "We should get together more often. We're always working."

"You work more than I do," Olivia told

her good-naturedly. "You need to get a life, Melissa O'Ballivan."

"I *have* a life, thank you very much," Melissa retorted, heading for Olivia's CD player and putting on some Christmas music. "Anyway, if anybody's going to preach to me about overdoing it at work and getting a life, it isn't going to be you, Big Sister."

"Are you dating anybody?" Olivia asked, opening one of the cartons of bubble lights. When they were younger, Big John had hung lights exactly like them on the family tree every year. Then they'd become a fire hazard, and he'd thrown them out.

"The last one ended badly," Melissa confessed, busy opening the ornament boxes and putting hangers through the little loops. So busy that she wouldn't meet Olivia's gaze.

"How so?"

"He was married," Melissa said. "Had me fooled, until the wife sent me a photo Christmas card showing them on a trip to the Grand Canyon last summer. Four kids and a dog."

"Yikes," Olivia said, wanting to hug Melissa, or at least lay a hand on her shoulder, but holding back. Her sister seemed uncharacteristically brittle, as though she might fall apart if anyone touched her just then. "You really cared about him, huh?"

"I cared," Melissa said. "What else is new? If there's a jerk within a hundred miles, I'll find him, rope him in and hand him my heart."

"Aren't you being a little hard on yourself?"

Melissa shrugged offhandedly. "The one before that wanted to meet Brad and present him with a demo so he could make it big in showbiz." She paused. "But at least *he* didn't have children."

"Mel, it happens. Cut yourself a little slack."

"You didn't see those kids. Freckles. Braces. They all looked so happy. And why not? How could they know their dad is a class-A, card-carrying schmuck?"

Once again Olivia found herself at a loss for words. She concentrated on clipping the lights to Charlie Brown's branches.

"Par-ump-pah-pum . . ." Bing Crosby sang from the CD player.

"I might as well tell you it's the talk of the family," Melissa said, picking up the conversational ball with cheerful determination, "that you skipped out of Thanksgiving to sneak off with Tanner Quinn."

Olivia stiffened. "I didn't 'sneak off' with

him," she said.

Not much, said her conscience.

"Don't be so defensive," Melissa replied, widening her eyes. "He's a hunk. I'd have left with him, too."

"It wasn't —"

"It wasn't what I think?" Melissa challenged, smiling now. "Of course it was. Are you in love with him?"

Olivia opened her mouth, closed it again.

Bing Crosby sang wistfully of orange groves and sunshine. He was dreaming of a white Christmas.

He could have hers.

"Are you?" Melissa pressed.

"No," Olivia said.

"Too bad," Melissa answered.

Olivia looked at her watch, pretending she hadn't heard that last remark. By now Brad was probably in the air, jetting toward Tennessee.

Hold on, Ashley, she thought. *Hold on.*

The call didn't come until almost midnight, and when it did, both Melissa and Olivia, snacking on leathery egg rolls snatched from the freezer and thawed in the oven, dived for the kitchen phone.

Olivia got there first. Home-court advantage.

"She's okay," Brad said. "We'll be back

203

sometime tomorrow."

"Put her on," Olivia replied anxiously.

"I don't think she's up to that right now," Brad answered.

"Tell her Melissa's here with me, and we'll be waiting when she gets home."

Brad agreed, and the call ended.

"She's all right, then?" Melissa asked carefully.

Olivia nodded, but she wasn't entirely convinced it was the truth. The only thing to do now was get some sleep — Melissa needed a night's rest, and so did she.

In her room, with Ginger sharing the bed, Olivia stared up at the ceiling and worried. Across the hall, in the tiny spare room, Melissa was probably doing the same thing.

Tanner, watching from his bedroom window, saw the lights go out across the field, in Olivia's house. He went to look in on Sophie and the puppies one more time, then showered, brushed his teeth, pulled on sweats and stretched out for the night.

Sleep proved elusive, and when it came, it was shallow, a partial unconsciousness ripe for lucid dreams. And not necessarily good ones.

He found himself in what looked like a hospital corridor, near the nurses' desk, and

204

when a tall, dark-haired woman came out of a room, wearing scrubs and carrying a chart, he thought it was Kat.

She was back, then. The last dream hadn't been a goodbye after all.

He tried to speak to her, but it was no use. He was no more articulate than the droopy Christmas garlands and greeting cards taped haphazardly to the walls and trimming the desk.

The general effect was forlorn, rather than festive.

The woman in scrubs slapped the chart down on the counter and sighed.

There were shadows under her eyes, and she was too thin. No wedding ring on her left hand, either.

"Nurse?" she called.

A heavy woman appeared from a back room. "Do you need something, Dr. Quinn?"

Dr. Quinn, medicine woman. It was a joke he and Sophie shared when they talked about her career plans.

Sophie. This was *Sophie* — some kind of ghost of Christmas future.

Tanner tried hard to wake up, but it didn't happen for him. During the effort, he missed whatever Sophie said in reply to the nurse's question.

"I thought you'd go home for Christmas this year," the nurse said chattily. "I'd swear I saw your name on the vacation list."

Sophie studied the chart, a little frown forming between her eyebrows. "I swapped with Dr. Severn," she answered distractedly. "He has a family."

Tanner felt his heart break. *You* have a family, Sophie, he cried silently.

"Anyway, my dad's overseas, building something," Sophie went on. "We don't make a big deal about Christmas."

Sophie, Tanner pleaded.

But she didn't hear him. She snapped the chart shut and marched off down the hospital corridor again, disappearing into a mist.

My dad's overseas, building something. We don't make a big deal about Christmas.

Sophie's words lingered in Tanner's head when he opened his eyes. He ran the back of his arm across his wet face, alone in the darkness.

So much for sleep.

CHAPTER NINE

Over what was left of the weekend, the snow melted and the roads were lined with muddy slush. It made the decorations on Main Street look as though they were trying just a shade too hard, by Olivia's calculations.

Brad and Ashley didn't get back to Stone Creek until Monday afternoon. Melissa and Olivia were waiting at Ashley's, along with Ginger, when Brad's truck pulled up outside. They'd considered turning on the outside lights to welcome Ashley home, but in the end it hadn't seemed like a good idea.

Olivia had brewed fresh coffee, though.

Melissa had brought a box of Ashley's favorite doughnuts from the bakery.

As they peered out the front window, watching as Brad helped Ashley out of the truck and held on to her arm as they approached the gate, both Olivia and Melissa knew coffee and doughnuts weren't going to be enough.

Ashley looked thinner — was that possible after only a couple of days? — and even from a distance, Olivia could see that there were deep shadows under her eyes.

Melissa rushed for the door and opened it as Brad brought Ashley up the steps. He shot a look of bruised warning at Melissa, then Olivia.

"I don't want to talk about it," Ashley said.

"You don't have to," Olivia told her softly, reaching for Ashley and drawing back when her sister flinched, huddled closer to Brad, as though she felt threatened. She wouldn't look at either Olivia or Melissa, but she did stoop to pat Ginger's head. "I just want to sleep."

Once Ashley was inside the house, Melissa urged her toward the stairs. The railing was buried under an evergreen garland.

"That must have been a very bad scene," Olivia said to Brad when the twins were on their way upstairs, followed by Ginger.

He nodded, his expression glum. Now that Olivia looked at him, she realized that he looked almost as bad as Ashley did.

"What happened?" Olivia prompted when her brother didn't say anything.

"She wouldn't tell me any more than she just told you." There was more, though. Olivia knew that, by Brad's face, even before he went on. "A desk clerk at Ashley's hotel told me she checked in, all excited, and a woman came to see her — the two of them met in the hotel restaurant for lunch. The woman was Mom, of course. She swilled a lot of wine, and things went sour, fast. According to this clerk, Mom started screaming that if she'd wanted 'a bunch of snot-nosed brats hanging off her,' she'd have stayed in Stone Creek and rotted."

The words, and the image, which she could picture only too well, struck Olivia like blows. It didn't help that she would have expected something similar out of any meeting with her mother.

"My God," she whispered. "Poor Ashley."

"It gets worse," Brad said. "Mom raised such hell in the restaurant that the police were called. Turns out she'd violated probation by getting drunk, and now she's in jail. Ashley's furious with me because I wouldn't bail her out."

A sudden headache slammed at Olivia's temples with such ferocity that she wondered if she was blowing a blood vessel in her brain. She nodded to let Brad know she'd heard, but her eyes were squeezed shut.

"I tried to get Ashley to stop at the doctor's office on the way into town a little while ago — maybe get some tranquilizers or something — but she said she just wanted to go home." He paused. "Liv, are you okay?"

"I've been better," she answered, opening her eyes. "Right now I'm not worried about myself. I should have known Ashley would have done something like this — tried to stop her —"

"It isn't your fault," Brad said.

Olivia nodded, but she probably wasn't very convincing, to Brad or herself.

"I've got to get home to Meg and the baby," Brad told her. "Can you and Melissa take it from here?"

Again Olivia nodded.

"You'll call if she seems to be losing ground?"

Olivia stood on tiptoe and kissed her brother's unshaven, wind-chilled cheek. "I'll call," she promised.

After casting a rueful glance toward the stairs, Brad turned and left.

Olivia was halfway up those same stairs when Melissa appeared at the top, a finger to her lips.

"She's resting," she whispered. Apparently Ginger had elected to stay in Ashley's room.

Together, Olivia and Melissa retreated to the kitchen.

"Did she say anything?" Olivia prodded.

"Just that it was terrible," Melissa replied, "and that she still doesn't want to talk about it."

Olivia's cell phone chirped. Great. After the slowest weekend on record, professionally speaking anyway, she was suddenly in demand.

"Dr. O'Ballivan," she answered, having seen the clinic's number on the ID panel.

"There's a horse colicking at the Wildes' farm," the receptionist, Becky, told her. "It's bad and Dr. Elliott is on call, but he's busy. . . ."

Colic. The ailment could be deadly for a horse. "I'm on my way," Olivia said.

"Go," Melissa said when she'd hung up. "I'll look after Ashley. Ginger, too."

Having no real choice, Olivia hurried out to the Suburban and headed for the Wildes'.

The next few hours were harrowing, with teenaged Sherry Wilde, the owner of the sick horse, on the verge of hysteria the whole time. Olivia managed to save the bay mare, but it was a fight.

She was so drained afterward that she pulled over and sat in the Suburban with her head resting on the steering wheel, once she'd driven out of sight of the house and barn, and cried.

211

Presently she heard another rig pull up behind her and, since she was about halfway between Stone Creek and Indian Rock, she figured it was Wyatt Terp or one of his deputies, out on patrol, stopping to make sure she was okay. Olivia sniffled inelegantly and lifted her head.

But the face on the other side of the window was Tanner's, not Wyatt's.

She hadn't seen him since supper at his place a few nights before.

He gestured for her to roll down the window.

She did.

"Engine trouble?" he asked.

Olivia shook her head. She must look a sight, she thought, with her eyes all puffy and her nose red enough to fly lead for Kris Kringle. She was a professional, good under pressure, and it was completely unlike her to sit sniveling beside the road.

"Move over," he said after locking his own vehicle by pressing a button on the key fob. "I'm driving."

"I'm all right — really . . ."

He already had the door open, and he was standing on the running board.

Olivia scrambled over the console to the passenger side once she realized he wasn't going to give in.

"Where to?" he asked.

"Home, I guess," Olivia said. She'd called the bed-and-breakfast before leaving the Wildes' farm, and Melissa had told her Ashley still wanted to be left alone. The family doctor had dropped by, at Brad's request, and given Ash a mild sedative.

Melissa planned to stay overnight.

"When you're ready to talk," Tanner said, checking the rearview mirror before pulling onto the road, "I'll be ready to listen."

"It might be a while," Olivia said, after a few moments spent struggling to get a grip. "Where's Sophie?"

Tanner grinned. "She stayed after school to watch the drama department rehearse for the winter play," he said. "We'll pick her up on our way if you don't mind."

It went without saying that Olivia didn't mind, but she said it anyway.

Sophie was waiting with friends when they pulled up in front of the middle school. She looked puzzled for a moment, then rushed, smiling, toward the Suburban.

"We really should go back and get your truck," Olivia fretted, glancing at Tanner as Sophie climbed into the rear seat.

"Maybe it will get dirty," Tanner said cheerfully. Then, when Olivia didn't smile, he added, "I'll send somebody from the construction crew to pick it up."

"Can we get pizza?" Sophie wanted to know.

"We have horses to feed," Tanner told her. "Not to mention Snidely and Whiplash. We'll order pizza after the chores are done."

"Our tree is all decorated," Sophie told Olivia. "You should come and see it."

"I will," Olivia said.

"Are you coming down with a cold?" Sophie wanted to know. "You sound funny."

"I'm all right," Olivia answered, touched.

They were about a mile out of town, on the far side of Stone Creek, when they spotted Ginger trudging alongside the road. Olivia's mouth fell open — she'd thought the dog was still at Ashley's.

"What's Ginger doing out here all alone?" Sophie demanded.

"I don't know," Olivia said, struggling in vain to open the passenger-side door even as Tanner stopped the Suburban, got out and lifted the weary dog off the ground. Carried her in his arms to the back of the rig and settled her on the blankets.

"I don't think she's hurt," Tanner said once he was behind the wheel again. "Just tired and pretty footsore."

A tear slipped down Olivia's cheek, and she wiped it away, but not quickly enough.

"Hey," he said, his voice husky. "It can't be that bad."

Olivia didn't answer.

Ashley would be all right.

Ginger would be, too.

But she wasn't so sure about herself.

At some point, without even realizing it, she'd fallen in love with Tanner Quinn. Talk about a dismal revelation.

Reaching her place, Tanner let Sophie stay behind with Olivia and Ginger while he went on to Starcross to feed Butterpie and Shiloh and see to the puppies, as well.

Holding off tears with everything she had, Olivia peeled off her vest, turned up the heat and gave Ginger a quick but thorough exam. Tanner's diagnosis had been correct — she was worn out, and she'd need some salve on the pads of her feet, but otherwise she was fine. "Why didn't you stay at Ashley's?" she asked. "I would have come back for you."

Ginger just looked up at her, eyes full of exhaustion and devoted trust.

"Can I order pizza?" Sophie asked, hovering by the phone.

Olivia smiled a fragile smile, nodded. *Keep busy,* she thought. *Keep busy.* She filled Ginger's water and kibble bowls and dragged her fluffy Ashley-made bed into the kitchen. Ginger turned a few circles and collapsed, obviously spent and blissfully happy to be home.

Sophie placed the pizza order and sat down cross-legged on the floor to pet Ginger, who slumbered on.

"Did Ginger run away?" she asked.

Olivia was making coffee. Maybe Santa would bring her a new percolator. Was it too late to write to him? Did he have an e-mail address?

Was she losing her ever-loving *mind?*

Yes, if she'd fallen for Tanner. He was as unavailable as Melissa's last guy.

"She and I were visiting my sister in town earlier," Olivia explained, amazed at how normal she sounded. "Ginger must have decided to come home on her own."

"I ran away once," Sophie confessed.

"So I heard," Olivia answered, listening more intently now. Watching the girl out of the corner of her eye.

"It was a stupid thing to do," Sophie elaborated.

"And dangerous," Olivia agreed.

"I just wanted to come home," Sophie said. "Like Ginger."

Olivia's throat thickened again. "How do you like Stone Creek Middle School?" she asked, forging bravely on. *Oh, and by the way, I'm hopelessly in love with your father.*

"They're doing *Our Town,* the week between Christmas and New Year's," Sophie said. "I would have tried out for the part of Emily if I lived here."

"They do *Our Town* every year," Olivia answered. "It's a tradition."

"Were you in it when you were in middle school?"

"No. I had stage fright. So I worked sets and costumes. But my older brother, Brad, had a leading role one year, and both my sisters, Ashley and Melissa, had parts when their turn came."

"You have stage fright?"

"I didn't get the show-business gene. That went to Brad."

"Dad has some of his CDs. I kind of like the way he sings."

"Me, too," Olivia said.

"Did you always want to be a veterinarian?"

Olivia left the coffeepot and sat down at the table, near Sophie and the sweetly slumbering Ginger. "For as long as I can remember," she said.

"I want to be a people doctor," Sophie said. "Like my mom was."

"I'm sure you'll be a good one."

Sophie looked very solemn, and she might

have been about to say something more about her mother, but the Suburban rolled noisily up alongside the house just then. A door slammed.

Tanner was back from feeding horses and puppies, and the pizza would be arriving soon, no doubt.

Maybe I'm over him, Olivia thought. *Maybe fighting for a horse's life made me overemotional.*

He knocked and came inside, shivering. Flecks of hay decorated his clothes. "It's cold out there," he said.

Nope, she wasn't over him.

Olivia's hand shook a little as she gestured toward the coffeepot. "Help yourself," she told him. She was ridiculously glad he was there, he and Sophie both.

Sophie got up from the floor while Tanner poured coffee, and wandered into the living room.

"Hey," she called right away. "Your little tree looks pretty good."

"Thanks," Olivia called back as she and Tanner exchanged low-wattage smiles.

I love you, Olivia said silently. *How's that for foolish?*

"How come there aren't any presents under it?"

"Soph," Tanner objected.

218

Sophie appeared in the doorway between the kitchen and living room.

"There are a lot of guys at our house, fixing up the barn," she told Olivia. "It's a good thing, too, because Aunt Tessa's horses will be tired when they get here."

"Are they on their way?" Olivia asked Tanner.

He nodded. "Tessa's bringing them herself," he said. "I wanted her to fly and let a transport company bring them, but she has a head as hard as Arizona bedrock."

"I think I'm going to like her," Olivia said.

Sophie beamed, nodding in agreement. "Once she's out here with us, she'll get over her break-up in no time!"

Olivia looked at Tanner. "Break-up?"

"Divorce," he said. "None of them are easy, but this one's a meat grinder."

"I'm sorry," Olivia told him, and she meant it. She remembered how broken up her dad had been after Delia skipped out. Knew only too well how *she* would feel when Tanner left Stone Creek for good.

"Can I plug in your Christmas tree?" Sophie asked.

"Sure," Olivia said.

Sophie disappeared again.

Tanner and Olivia looked at each other in silence.

Mercifully, the pizza delivery guy broke the spell by honking his car horn from the driveway.

Tanner grinned and started for the door.

"My turn to provide supper," Olivia said, easing past him.

When she came back with the goods, snow-speckled and wishing she'd taken the time to put on her coat, Tanner was setting the table.

Ginger roused herself long enough to sniff the air. Pizza was one of her favorites, although Olivia never gave her more than a few bites.

Supper was almost magical — they might have been a family, Tanner and Olivia and Sophie, talking around the table as they ate in the warm, cozy kitchen.

Sophie snuck a few morsels to Ginger, and Olivia pretended not to see.

Because Tanner's truck had been picked up and driven to Starcross, Olivia gave her neighbors a ride home when the time came. She waited until they'd both gone inside, after waving from the porch, and watched as the tree lights sprang to life in the front window.

Sophie's doing, she supposed.

On the way back to her place, because she still wanted to cry, Olivia called Ashley's house again.

"She's fine, mother hen," Melissa told her. "I talked her into having some soup a little while ago, and a cup of tea, too. She says she'll be her old self again after a bubble bath."

Olivia's relief was so great that she didn't ask if anybody had noticed Ginger's escape. Nor, of course, did she announce that she was in love.

"I can't seem to find the dog, though," Melissa said. "It's a big house. She must be here somewhere."

"She's home," Olivia said.

"You picked her up?"

"She walked."

"Oh, God, Livie, I'm sorry — she must have slipped out through Ashley's pet door in the laundry room —"

"Ginger's fine," Olivia assured her worried sister.

"Thank God," Melissa replied. "Why do you suppose she put in a pet door — Ashley, I mean — when she doesn't have a *pet?*"

"Maybe she wants one."

"I could stop by the shelter and adopt a kitten for her or something."

"Don't you dare," Olivia said. "Adopting an animal is a commitment, and Ashley has to make that decision on her own."

"Okay, Dr. Dolittle," Melissa teased. "*Okay.* Spare me the responsible pet owner lecture, all right? I was just thinking out loud."

"Why don't *you* adopt a dog or a cat?"

"I'm allergic, remember?" Melissa answered, giving a sneeze right on cue. It was the first sign of Melissa's hypochondria that Olivia had seen in recent days.

"Right," Olivia replied.

By then the snow was coming down so thick and fast, she could barely see her driveway. *Please God,* she prayed silently, *no emergencies tonight.*

She and Melissa swapped goodbyes, and she ended the call.

A nice hot bubble bath didn't sound half-bad, she thought when the cold air hit her as she got out of the Suburban. Maybe she'd light a few candles, put on her snuggly robe after the bath, make cocoa and watch something Christmasy and sentimental on TV.

Talk herself out of loving a no-strings-attached kind of man.

Ginger got up when she came in, ate a few kibbles and immediately headed for the back door.

So much for getting warm.

Olivia went outside with the dog.

"It's not as if I plan to run away, you know," Ginger remarked.

Through the storm, Olivia could just make out the lights over at Starcross. The sight comforted her and, at the same time, made her feel oddly isolated.

"I wouldn't have thought you'd try to walk all the way home from Stone Creek," Olivia scolded. "Ginger, it's at least five miles."

"I made it, didn't I?" Having completed her outside enterprise, Ginger headed for the back porch, stopping to shake off the snow before going on into the kitchen.

Olivia tromped in after her, hugging herself. Shut the door and locked it.

"I'm taking a bubble bath," she said. "Don't bother me unless you're bleeding or the place catches fire."

Ginger took hold of her dog bed with her teeth and hauled it into the living room, in front of the tree. In the softer light, Charlie Brown looked almost — well — *bushy.* Downright festive, even.

She'd unplugged the bubble lights before leaving to take Tanner and Sophie home. Now she bent to plug them in again, waited until the colorful liquid in the little glass vials began to bubble cheerfully.

She immediately thought of Big John, but tonight the memory of her grandfather didn't hurt. She smiled, remembering what a big deal he'd always made over Christmas, spending money he probably didn't have, taking them all up into the timber country to look for just the right tree, sitting proud and straight backed in the audience at each new production of *Our Town.* In retrospect, she knew he'd been trying to make up for the losses in their lives — hers, Brad's, Ashley's and Melissa's.

The year Brad was in the play, Ashley had cried all the way home to the ranch. Big John had carried her into the house and demanded to know what the "waterworks" were all about.

"All those dead people sitting in folding chairs!" Ashley had wailed. "Is Daddy someplace like that, all in shadow, sitting in a folding chair?"

Big John's face had been a study in manfully controlled emotion. "No, honey," he'd said gruffly, there in the kitchen at Stone Creek Ranch, while Brad and Olivia and Melissa peeled out of their coats. "*Our Town* is just a story. Your daddy isn't sitting around in a folding chair, and you can take that to the bank. He's too busy riding horses, I figure. The way I figure it, they've got some mighty good trails up there in heaven, and there aren't any shadows to speak of, either."

Ashley's eyes had widened almost to saucer size, but she'd stopped crying. "How do you know, Big John?" she'd asked, gazing up at him. "Is it in the Bible?"

Brad, a pretty typical teenager, had given a snort at that.

Big John had quelled him with a look. "No," he told Ashley, resting a hand on her shoulder. "It probably isn't in the Bible. But there are some things that just make sense. How many cowboys would want to go to heaven if there weren't any horses to ride?"

Ashley had brightened at the question. In her child's mind, the argument made sense.

Blinking, Olivia returned to the present moment.

"Time for that hot bath I promised myself," she told Ginger.

"I wouldn't mind one either," Ginger said.

And so it was that Olivia bathed the dog first, toweled her off and then scrubbed out the tub for her own turn.

When she finished, she put on flannel pajamas and her favorite bathrobe and padded out to the living room.

Ginger had the TV on, watching *Animal Planet.*

"How did you do that?" Olivia asked. There were some things that strained even an animal communicator's credulity.

"If you step on the remote just right, it happens," Ginger replied.

"Oh, good grief," Olivia said, glancing in Charlie Brown's direction.

"I wouldn't have thought he could look that good," Ginger observed, following Olivia's gaze.

She reclaimed the remote. Checked the channel guide.

"We're watching *The Bishop's Wife*," she told Ginger.

Ginger didn't protest. She liked Cary Grant, too.

"After it's over," the dog said, *"we can talk about how you're in love with Tanner."*

"I don't want to talk about it," Ashley said, for the fourth or fifth time, the next morning when Olivia stopped by her house on the way to the clinic, Ginger in tow. Melissa had already gone to work.

Olivia was still in love, but she was adjusting.

"Fair enough," she replied. Ashley looked almost like her old self, and she was expecting paying guests later in the day. Rolling out piecrusts in preparation for some serious baking.

Some people drank when they were upset.

Others chain-smoked.

Ashley baked.

"Tell me about the guests," Olivia said, trying to snitch a piece of pie dough and getting her hand slapped for her trouble.

"They're long-term," Ashley answered, rolling harder, so the flour flew. Some of it was in her hair, and a lot more decorated her holly-sprigged chef's apron. "Tanner Quinn called and booked the rooms. He said he needed space for four people, and he'd vouch for their character because they all work for him."

Olivia raised an eyebrow. "I see," she said, considering another attempt at the pie dough and doing a pretty good job of hiding the fact that Tanner's name made the floor tremble under her feet.

"Don't even think about it," Ashley said, sounding like her old self. *Almost* her old self, anyway. She was still pretty ragged around the edges, but if she didn't want to talk about their mother just yet, Olivia would respect that.

Even if it killed her.

"Nice of him," she said. "Tanner, I mean. He could have put the crew up at the Sundowner Motel, or over in Indian Rock."

Ashley pounded at the pie dough and rolled vigorously again. It looked like a good upper-arm workout. "All I know is they're paying top dollar, and they'll be here until next spring. Merry Christmas to me. For a few months, anyway, I won't need any more 'loans' from Brad to keep the business going."

Olivia didn't miss the slight edge in her sister's voice. "Ash," she said. "This will get easier. I promise it will."

"I should have listened to you."

"But you didn't, and that's okay. You're a grown woman, with a perfect right to make your own decisions."

"She's *horrible,* Liv."

"Let it go, Ash."

"Do you know why she was on probation? For shoplifting, and writing bad checks, and — and God knows what else."

"Brad said you were miffed because he wouldn't bail her out."

Ashley set down the rolling pin, backed away from the counter. Flour drifted down onto Ginger's head like finely sifted snow. "He was right," Ashley said. "He was right not to bail that — that *woman* out!"

"I can stay if you want me to," Olivia said.

Ashley shook her head, hard. "No," she insisted. "But I wouldn't mind if Ginger were here to keep me company."

Olivia looked at Ginger. Knew instantly

that she wanted to stay.

"Don't you dare try to walk home again," she told the dog. "I'll pick you up after I finish my last call."

"Oh, for Pete's sake," Ashley said. Like Brad and Melissa, she had always taken the Dr. Dolittle thing with a grain of salt. Make that a barrel. Only Big John had really understood — he'd said his grandmother could talk to animals, too.

"Later," Olivia said, and dashed out through the back, though she did stop briefly to secure the latch on the pet door, in case Ginger got another case of wanderlust.

Now that he had crews working, the shelter project took off. The barn at Starcross was coming along nicely, too. Tanner was pleased.

Or he *should* have been.

Sophie loved school — specifically Stone Creek Middle School. She'd already found some friends, and she was making good progress at house-training the puppies, too. She did her chores without being asked, exercising Butterpie every day.

That morning, when he came back inside from feeding the horses, she was already making breakfast.

"I used your laptop," she'd confessed immediately.

"Is that why you're trying to make points?"

Sophie had laughed. "Nope. I had to check my e-mail. All hell's breaking loose at Briarwood."

He hadn't been surprised to hear that, since he'd called both Jack McCall and Ms. Wiggins soon after the drug conversation with Sophie that day in the truck, and read them every line of the riot act, twice over.

Ms. Wiggins had promised a thorough and immediate investigation.

Jack had asked if he was sure Sophie wasn't playing him, so she could stay with him in Stone Creek.

"I *really* can't go back there now, Dad," Sophie had told him, turning serious again. "Everybody knows I'm the one who blew the whistle, and that won't win me the Miss Popularity pin."

He'd ruffled her hair. "Don't worry about it. You'll be going to a new school, anyway." He'd found a good one in Phoenix, just over two hours away by car, but he was saving the details for a surprise. He wanted Tessa to be there when he broke the good news, and Olivia, too, if possible.

Olivia.

Now, there was a gift he'd like to unwrap again.

As soon as Tessa got there and he had somebody to hold down the fort with Sophie, he was going to ask Olivia O'Ballivan, DVM, out on a real date. Take her to dinner somewhere fancy, up in Flagstaff, or in nearby Sedona.

In the meantime, he'd have to tough it out. Work hard. Take a lot of cold showers.

A worker went by, whistling "Have Yourself a Merry Little Christmas."

Tanner almost told him to shut the hell up.

CHAPTER TEN

There was no slowing down Christmas. It was bearing down on Stone Creek at full throttle, hell-bent-for-election, as Big John used to say. Watering Charlie Brown in her living room before braving snowy roads to get to the clinic for a full day of appointments, Olivia hummed a carol under her breath.

The week since Ashley had come home from Tennessee had been a busy one, rushing by. Olivia had had supper with Sophie and Tanner twice, once at her place, once at theirs.

And she hadn't been able to shake off loving him.

It was for real.

The big tree in the center of town would be lighted as soon as the sun went down that night, to the noisy delight of the whole community, and after that, over at the high school gymnasium, the chamber of commerce was throwing their annual Christmas carnival, with a dance to follow.

In the kitchen Ginger began to bark.

Olivia frowned and went to investigate. They'd already been outside, and she hadn't heard anybody drive in.

Passing the kitchen window, she saw a late-model truck pulling in at Starcross, pulling a long, mud-splashed horse trailer behind it.

Sophie's much-anticipated aunt Tessa, Tanner's sister, had finally arrived. That would be a relief to Tanner — more than once over the past week he'd admitted he was on the verge of heading out to look for Tessa. Even though Tessa called every night, according to Sophie, to report her progress, Tanner had been jumpy.

"He worries a lot about what *could happen*," Sophie had told Olivia, on the q.t., while the two of them were frying chicken in the kitchen at Starcross. Then, as if concerned that Olivia might be turned off by the admission, she'd added, "But he's *really* brave. He saved Uncle Jack's life *twice* in the Gulf War."

"And modest, too," Olivia had teased.

But Sophie's expression was serious. "Uncle Jack told me about it," she'd said. "Not Dad."

Now, with Ginger barking fit to deafen her, Olivia made an executive decision. She'd stop by Starcross on the way to town and offer a brief welcome to Tessa. It was the neighborly thing to do, after all.

And if she was more than a little curious about the soon-to-be-divorced former TV star, well, nothing wrong with that. Brad would have to share his local-celebrity status, at least temporarily.

Showing up would be an intrusion of sorts, though, Olivia reasoned as she and Ginger slipped and slid down the icy drive-way to the main road. Who knew what kind of shape Tessa Quinn Whoever might be in after driving practically across country with a load of horses and a broken heart?

All the more reason to offer a friendly greeting, Olivia decided.

Tanner had probably already left for the construction site in town, and Sophie was surely in school, secretly lusting after the role of Emily in next year's production of *Our Town.* Stone Creek never got tired of that play — perhaps because it reminded them to be grateful for ordinary blessings.

It bothered Olivia to think Tessa might have no one to welcome her, help her unload her prized horses and settle them into stalls. Since all her morning appointments were things a veterinary assistant could handle, Olivia decided she'd offer whatever assistance she could.

Only, Tanner was there when Olivia arrived, and so was Sophie.

She and Tessa — a tall, dark-haired woman who resembled Tanner — were just breaking up a hug. Tanner was pulling out the ramp on the horse trailer, but he stopped and smiled as Olivia drove up.

Her heart beat double time.

Sophie was obviously filling Tessa in on the new arrival as Olivia got out of the Suburban, leaving Ginger behind in the passenger seat. Tessa's wide-set gray eyes, friendly but reserved, too, took Olivia's measure as she approached, hands in the pockets of her down vest.

What, if anything, Olivia wondered, had Tanner told his sister about the veterinarian-next-door?

Nothing, Olivia hoped. And everything.

Except for a few stolen kisses when Sophie happened to be out of range, nothing had happened between Olivia and Tanner since Thanksgiving.

For all that she was playing with fire and she knew it, Olivia was past ready for another round of hot sex with the first man she'd ever loved — and probably the last.

Tanner made introductions; Tessa wiped her palms down the slim thighs of her gray corduroy pants before offering Olivia a handshake. The caution lingered in her eyes, though, and she slipped an arm around Sophie's shoulders after the hellos had been said, and pulled her against her side.

"I'm trying to talk Tessa into going to the tree-lighting and the Christmas carnival and dance tonight," Tanner said, watching his sister with an expression of fond, worried relief. "So far, it's no-go."

"It's been a long drive," Tessa said, smiling somewhat feebly. "I'd rather stay here. Maybe I'll stop feeling as if the road is still rolling under me."

"I'll stay with you," Sophie told her aunt, clinging with both arms and looking up with a delight that made Olivia feel an unbecoming rush of envy. "We can order pizza."

"You don't want to miss the tree-lighting," Tessa said to Sophie, squeezing her once and kissing the top of her head. "Or the carnival. *That* sounds like a lot of fun." The woman looked almost shell-shocked, the way Ashley had when Brad brought her home from Tennessee, and it wasn't because of the endless highways and roadside hotels.

Will I look like that when Tanner's gone? Olivia asked herself, even though she already knew the answer.

"Dad could bring me back after," Sophie insisted. "Couldn't you, Dad?"

Tanner looked at Olivia.

Tessa's glance bounced between the two of them.

"Are you up for a Christmas dance, Doc?" Tanner asked. It was a simple question, but it sounded grave under the watchful eyes of Tessa and Sophie.

"I guess so," Olivia said, because jumping up and down and shouting "Yes, yes, yes!" would have given her away.

"Note the wild enthusiasm," Tanner said, grinning.

"I *think* she said yes," Tessa remarked, her smile warming noticeably.

"Do you have a dress?" Sophie inquired, her brow furrowed. Clearly she was worried that Olivia would skip off to the Christmas festivities in her customary cow-doctor getup.

"Maybe I'll buy one," Olivia said, after chuckling. She still felt as if she'd swallowed a handful of jumping beans, though.

Buying a dress she'd probably never wear again? *What I did for love.*

When she was a creaky old spinster veterinarian, she'd show the dress to her brother's and sisters' kids and tell them the story. The

G-rated part, anyway.

She checked her watch, which was a perfectly normal thing to do. She even smiled. "I guess I'd better get to the clinic," she said. Then, achingly aware of Tanner standing at the edge of her vision, she added, "Unless you need some help unloading those horses?"

"I think I can handle it, Doc," he said good-naturedly. "But if you're in a favor-doing mood, you can drop Sophie off at school."

"Sure," Olivia said, pleased.

"I thought I'd take today off," Sophie piped up.

"You're in or you're out, kiddo," Tanner told her. "You were dead set on continuing your education, remember?"

"Go," Tessa told her niece. "I'll probably be asleep all day anyway."

Sophie nodded, very reluctantly, but in that quicksilver way of children, she had a warm smile going by the time she climbed into the front seat of the Suburban. Ginger, always accommodating, when it came to Sophie, anyway, had already moved to the back, her big furry head blocking the rear-view mirror.

"Where are you going to plant Charlie Brown when Christmas is over?" Sophie

238

asked, snapping her seat belt into place and settling in.

"I hadn't thought about it," Olivia admitted. "Maybe in town, on the grounds of the new shelter. I'll be living upstairs when it's finished."

"I wish all Christmas trees came in pots, so they could be planted afterward," Sophie said. "That way, they wouldn't die."

"Me, too," Olivia said.

"Do you think trees have feelings?"

Ginger had shifted just enough to allow Olivia a glance in the rearview. Olivia caught a glimpse of Tanner, leading the first horse down the ramp and toward the newly refurbished barn.

"I don't know," Olivia answered belatedly, "but they're living things, and they deserve good treatment."

Mercifully, the conversation took a different track after that, though the subject of trees lingered in Olivia's mind, leading to Kris Kringle at the lot in town, and finally to Rodney, who was living the high life in Brad's barn at Stone Creek Ranch. For that little stretch of time, she didn't think about Tanner.

Much.

"Aunt Tessa is pretty, don't you think?" Sophie asked as ramshackle country fences whizzed by on both sides of the Suburban.

"She certainly is," Olivia agreed, feeling unusually self-conscious about her clothes and her bobbed hair. Tessa's locks flowed, wavy and almost as dark as Tanner's, past her shoulders. "I don't recall seeing her on TV, though."

"We got you the season one DVD of *California Women* for Christmas," Sophie said with a spark of mischief in her eyes. "It was supposed to be a surprise, though."

Sophie and Tanner had bought her a Christmas present?

Lord, what was she going to give them in return? She hadn't even shopped for Mac yet, let alone Brad and Meg, Ashley and Melissa, and the office staff and the other vets she worked with at the clinic.

"It's no big deal," Sophie assured her, evidently reading her expression.

Fruitcake? Olivia wondered, distracted. One of those things that came in a colorful tin and had a postapocalyptic sell-by date? If they didn't eat it, it could double as a doorstop.

"How come you're frowning like that?" Sophie pressed.

"I'm just thinking," Olivia said as they reached the outskirts of town. The hardware store had fruitcake; she'd seen a display when she bought the lights and ornaments for Charlie Brown.

And what kind of loser bought bakery goods in a hardware store?

This was a job for super-Ashley, she of the wildly wielded rolling pin and the flour-specked hair. Olivia would drop in on her on her lunch break, she decided, to (a) borrow a dress for the dance, thereby saving posterity from the tale, and (b) persuade her sister to whip up something impressive for the Quinns' Christmas present.

"This is cool," Sophie said a few minutes later when Olivia pulled up to the curb in front of Stone Creek Middle School. "Almost like having a mom." Having dropped that one, she turned to say a quick goodbye to Ginger, and then she disappeared into the gaggle of kids milling on the lawn.

Olivia's hands trembled on the steering wheel as she eased out of a tangle of leaving and arriving traffic.

"We still have half an hour before you're due at the clinic," Ginger said, brushing Olivia's face with her plumy tail as she returned to the front seat. *"Let's go by the tree lot and have a word with Kris Kringle. For Rodney's sake, we need to know he's on the level."*

"Not going to happen," Olivia said firmly. "I've got some paperwork to catch up on before I start seeing patients and, besides, Kringle checked out with Indian Rock PD. Plus, Rodney's doing okay at the home-place. I get daily reports from either Meg or Brad, and we've been to visit our reindeer buddy twice in the last three days."

Ginger was determined to be helpful, apparently. Or just to butt in. *"How's your mother?"*

"I do not want to talk about my mother."

"Denial," Ginger accused. *"Sooner or later, you're going to have to see her, just to get closure."*

"You need to stop watching talk-TV while I'm at work," Olivia said. "Besides, Mommy dearest is in the clink right now."

"No, she isn't. Brad got her a lawyer and had her moved to a swanky 'recovery center' in Flagstaff."

Olivia almost ran the one red light in Stone Creek. "How do you know these things?"

"Rodney told me the last time we visited. He heard Brad and Meg talking about it in the barn."

"And you're just getting around to mentioning this now?"

"I knew you wouldn't take it well. And there's the being in love with Tanner thing."

Olivia grabbed her cell phone and speed-dialed her sneaky brother. Mr. Tough, refusing to bail their mom out of the hoosegow back in Tennessee. He hadn't said a single word to her about bringing Delia to Arizona, or to the twins, either. They'd have told her if he had.

"Is Mom in a treatment center in Flagstaff?" she demanded the moment Brad said hello.

"How did you know that?" Brad asked, sounding both baffled and guilty.

"Never mind how I know. I just do."

Brad heaved a major sigh. "Okay. Yes. Mom's in Flagstaff. I was going to tell you and the twins after Christmas."

"Why the change of heart, Brad?" Olivia snapped, annoyed for the obvious reason and, also, because Ginger was right. If she wanted any closure, she'd have to visit her mother, and after what had happened to Ashley, the prospect had all the appeal of locking herself in a cage with a crazed grizzly bear.

"She's our mother," Brad said after a long silence. "I wanted to turn my back on her, the way she turned hers on us, but in the end I couldn't do it."

Olivia's eyes stung. Good thing she was pulling into the clinic lot, because she couldn't see well enough to drive at the moment. "I know you did the right thing," she said as Ginger nudged her shoulder sympathetically. "But I'll be a while getting used to the idea of Mom living right up the road, after all these years."

"Tell me about it," Brad said. "It's a long-term thing, Liv. Basically, the prognosis for her recovery isn't good."

Olivia sat very still in the Suburban, nosed up to the wall of the clinic, clutching the phone so tightly in her right hand that her knuckles ached. "Are you telling me she's dying?"

"We're all dying," Brad answered. "I'm telling you that, in this case, 'treatment center' is a euphemism for one of the best mental hospitals in the world. She could live to be a hundred, but she'll probably never leave Palm Haven."

"She's crazy?"

"She's fried her brain, between the booze and snorting a line of coke whenever she could scrape the money together. So, yeah. *She's crazy.*"

"Oh, God."

"They're adjusting her medication, and she'll eat regularly, anyway. I'm not planning to pay her a visit until sometime after the first, and I'd suggest you wait, too. This is Mac's first Christmas, and I plan to enjoy it."

Becky, the receptionist, beckoned from the side door of the clinic.

"I've got to go," Olivia said, nodding to Becky that she'd be right in. "Will you and Meg be at the tree-lighting and all that?"

"Definitely the tree-lighting. Probably the carnival, too. But maybe not the dance. Mac's getting a tooth, so he's not his usual sunny self."

Olivia laughed, blinked away tears.

This was life, she supposed. Their mother's tragedy on the one hand, a baby having his first Christmas and sprouting teeth on the other.

Falling in love with the wrong man at the wrong time.

What could you do but tough it out?

The Sophie-of-Christmas-future haunted Tanner — she still came to him almost every night in his dreams, and of course he mulled them over during the days. In one memorable visit he'd found her living alone in an expensive but sparsely furnished apartment, with only a little ceramic tree to mark the presence of a holiday. He'd counted two Christmas cards tacked to her wall. In another, she tried to get through to him by phone, wanting to wish him a Merry Christmas. He'd been unreachable. And in a third installment he'd seen her standing wistfully at the edge of a city playground, watching a flock of young mothers and their children skating on a frozen pond.

Was this really a glimpse of the future, Ebenezer Scrooge–style, or was he just torturing himself with parental guilt?

Either way, he'd come to dread closing his eyes at night.

"Sophie looks happy," Tessa remarked from her seat at the kitchen table. Now that she'd finally arrived safely at Starcross at least, Tanner had one fewer thing to worry about. "And I like Olivia. Something special going on between the two of you?"

"What makes you think that?" he asked, hedging.

Tessa smiled at him over the rim of her coffee cup. "Oh, maybe the way you sort of held your breath when you asked her to the dance, until she said yes, and the way she blushed —"

"If I remember correctly," Tanner broke in, "she said 'I guess so.' "

"Could it be you're finally thinking of settling down, Big Brother?"

Tanner dragged back a chair and sat. "A week ago, even a *day* ago, I probably would have said no. Emphatically. But I'm getting pretty worried about Sophie."

Tessa arched an eyebrow, waited in silence.

"I've been having these crazy dreams," he confessed, after a few moments spent trying to convince himself that Tessa would think he was nuts if he told her about them.

"What kind of crazy dreams?" Tessa asked gently, pushing her coffee cup aside, folding her arms and resting them on the table's edge.

Tanner shoved a hand through his hair. "It's as if I travel through time," he admitted, every word torn out of him like a strip of hide. "Sophie's in her thirties, and she's a doctor, but she's alone in the world."

"Hmmm," Tessa said. "The doctor is in. Advice, five cents."

Tanner gave a raw chuckle. "Put it on my bill," he said.

"How do you fit into these dreams?"

"I'm off building something, in some other part of the world. At the same time, I'm there somehow, watching Sophie. And who knows where you are. I don't want to scare you or anything, but you haven't been a guest star."

"Go on," Tessa said.

"I love my daughter, Tessa," Tanner said.

"I don't want her to end up — well, alone like that."

Tessa's gray eyes widened, and a smile flicked at the corner of her mouth. She was still beautiful, and she still got acting offers, but she always turned them down because it would mean leaving her horses. "Sophie's been miserable at boarding school," she said. "Last fall, when it was time for her to go back, she begged me to let her stay on with me at the farm. I wanted so much to say yes, and damn *your* opinion in the matter, but things were going downhill fast between Paul and me even then. She'd heard us fighting all summer, and I knew it wasn't good for her."

"I thought she was *safe* at school."

" 'Thought'? Past tense? What's happened, Tanner?"

Briefly Tanner explained what Sophie had told him about the easy availability of meth and ice at Briarwood. "It's not like Stone Creek is Brigadoon or anything." He sighed. "A kid can probably score any kind of drug right here in rural America. But I really thought I had all the bases covered."

"Give Sophie a little credit," Tessa said, and though her tone was firm, she reached across the table to touch Tanner's hand. "She's way too smart to do drugs."

"I know," Tanner answered. "But I've always thought she'd be happy when she grew up — that she'd come to understand that I had her best interests at heart, sending her away to school. . . ."

"And the dreams made you question that?"

Tanner nodded. "They're so — so *real*, Tess. I can't shake the feeling that Sophie's going to have no life outside her work — all because she doesn't know how to be part of a family."

"Heavy stuff," Tessa said. "Are you in love with Olivia?"

"I don't know what I feel," Tanner answered, after a long silence. "And I don't necessarily have to get married to give Sophie a home, do I? I could sell off the overseas part of the business, or just close it down. I'd still have to do some traveling, but if you were here —"

"Hold it," Tessa broke in. "I can't promise I'm going to stay, Tanner. And one way or the other, I don't intend to live off your generosity like some poor relation."

"You won't have to," Tanner said. "There's money, Tess. Kat and I set it aside for you a long time ago."

Tessa's cheeks colored up. Her pride was kicking in, just as Tanner had known it would. *"What?"*

"You put me through college on what you earned when you were acting, Tessa," he reminded her. "You took care of Gram while I was in the service and then getting the business started. You're *entitled* to all the help I can give you."

Tessa went from pink to pale. Her eyes narrowed. "I can provide for myself," she said.

"Can you?" Tanner countered. "Good for you. Because that's more than I could do when I was in college and for a long time after that, and it's more than Gram could have managed, too, with just her Social Security and the take from that roadside vegetable stand of hers."

"How *much* money, Tanner?"

"Enough," Tanner said. He got up, walked to the small desk in the corner of the kitchen and jerked a bound folder out of the drawer. Returning to the table, he tossed it down in front of her.

Tessa opened the portfolio and stared at the figures, her eyes rounding at all those zeroes.

"The magic of compound interest," Tanner said.

"This money should be Sophie's," Tessa whispered, her voice thin and very soft. "My

God, Tanner, this is a *fortune.*"

"Sophie has a trust fund. I started it with Kat's life insurance check, and the last time I looked, it was around twice that much."

Tessa swallowed, looked up at him in shock, momentarily speechless.

"You can draw on it, or let it grow. My accountant has the tax angle all figured out, and it's in my name until the divorce is final, so Paul can't touch it." Still standing, Tanner folded his arms. "It's up to you, Tess. You're real good at giving. How are you at *receiving?*"

Tessa huffed out a stunned breath. "I could buy out Paul's half of the horse farm —"

"*Or* you could start over, right here, with a place of your own. No bad memories attached. Times are hard, and there are a lot of good people looking to sell all or part of their land."

"I can't think. Tanner, this is — this is unbelievable! I knew you were doing well, but I had no idea . . ."

"I'm late," he said.

On his way out, he checked on the puppies, found them sleeping in their box by the stove, curled up together as if they were still in the womb. They were so small, so helpless, so wholly trusting.

251

His throat tightened as he took his coat off the peg on the wall by the back door. He couldn't help drawing a parallel between the pups and Sophie.

"I'll be at the job site in town," he said. "You have my cell number if you need anything."

Tessa was still hunched over the portfolio. Her shoulders were shaking a little, so Tanner figured she was crying, though he couldn't be sure, with her back to him and all.

"Will you be okay here alone?" he asked gruffly.

She nodded vigorously, but didn't turn around to meet his gaze.

That damnable pride again.

Grabbing up his truck keys from the counter, he left the house. It was snowing so hard by then, he figured he'd probably let the construction crew off an hour or two early.

And Olivia had agreed to go to the dance with him that night.

It wasn't quite the date he'd had in mind, but she was planning to wear a dress, and Tessa would be on hand to keep an eye on Sophie after the tree-lighting and the carnival.

This was shaping up to be a half-decent

Christmas.

Climbing behind the wheel of the truck, Tanner started the engine, whistling "Jingle Bells" under his breath, and headed for town.

Ashley, with the help of a few very tall elves in college sweatshirts, was on a high ladder decorating her annual mongo Christmas tree when Olivia and Ginger showed up at noon.

"I need to borrow a dress for the dance," Olivia said.

"Hello to you, too," Ashley replied. She still looked a little feeble, but she was obviously into the holiday spirit, or she wouldn't have been decking the halls. And if she had a clue that Delia was in Flagstaff, luxuriously hospitalized, it didn't show. "I'm taller than you are. Anything I loaned you would have to be hemmed. I don't have time for that, and you can't sew."

"I sew all the time. It's called surgery. Ashley, this is an emergency. Can I raid your closet? Please? The hardware store doesn't sell dresses, and I don't have time to drive up to Flagstaff and shop."

Ashley waved her toward the stairs. "Anything but the blue velvet number with the little beads. I'm wearing that myself."

Olivia wiggled her eyebrows. Ginger snugged herself up on the hooked rug in front of the crackling blaze in the fireplace and relaxed into a power nap. That dog was at home anywhere. And everywhere.

"You have a date?" Olivia asked.

"As a matter of fact, I do," Ashley replied, carefully draping a single strand of tinsel over a branch. She'd do that two jillion times, to make the tree look perfect. "It's a blind date, if you must know. A friend of Tanner Quinn's — he's going to be staying here. The friend, not Tanner."

Olivia paused at the base of the stairway. "I hope it goes well," she said. "It could be awkward living under the same roof with a bad date until next spring."

"Thanks a heap, Liv. Now I'm *twice* as nervous."

Olivia hurried up the stairs. She still had to broach the subject of Ashley whipping up something spectacular for her to give Tanner, Sophie and Tessa for Christmas. An ice castle, made of sugar, she thought. Failing that, fancy cookies would work — the kind with colored frosting and sugar sparkles.

But the outfit had to come first.

Ashley's room was almost painfully tidy — the bed made, all the furniture matching, the prints tastefully arranged on the pale pink walls. Everywhere she looked, there was lace, or ruffles, or both.

It was almost impossible to imagine a man in that room.

Olivia sighed, thinking of her own jumbled bed, liberally sprinkled with dog hair. Her clothes were all over the floor, and she hadn't seen the surface of the dresser in weeks.

Yikes. If the date with Tanner went the way she hoped it would, she'd wish she'd spruced the place up a little — but at least he wouldn't have to contend with lace and ruffles.

She would cut out of the clinic an hour early that afternoon, assuming there were no disasters in the interim. Run the vacuum cleaner, dust a little, change the sheets.

She turned her mind back to the task at hand. Ashley's closet was jammed, but organized. Even color coded, for heaven's sake. Olivia swiped a pair of black velvet palazzo pants — probably gaucho pants on Ashley — and tried them on. If she rolled them up at the waist and wore her high-heeled boots, she probably wouldn't catch a toe in a hem and fall on her face.

A red silk tank top and a glittering silver shawl completed the ensemble.

Piece of cake, Olivia thought smugly,

heading out of the room and back down the stairs with the garments draped over one arm.

At the bottom of the steps, just opening her mouth to pitch the sugar-ice-castle idea to Ashley, she stopped in her tracks.

A guy stood just inside the front door, and what a guy he was. Military haircut, hard body, straight back and shoulders. Wearing black from head to foot. Only the twinkle in his hazel eyes as he looked up at Ashley saved him from looking like a CIA agent trying to infiltrate a terrorist cell.

Ashley, staring back at him, seemed in imminent danger of toppling right off the ladder.

The air sizzled.

"Jack McCall," Ashley marveled. "You son of a bitch!"

CHAPTER ELEVEN

Jack McCall grinned and saluted. "Good to see you again, Ash," he said, admiring her with a sweep of his eyes. "Are we still going to the dance together tonight?"

Ashley shinnied down the ladder, which was no mean trick in a floor-length Laura Ashley jumper. "I wouldn't go *anywhere* with you, you jerk," she cried. "Get out of my house!"

Olivia's mouth fell open. Ashley was the consummate bed-and-breakfast owner. She *never* screamed at guests — and Mr. McCall was clearly a guest, since he had a suitcase — much less called them sons of bitches.

"Sorry," McCall said, crossing his eyes a little at the finger Ashley was about to shake under his nose. "The deal's made, the lease is signed and I'm here until spring. On and off."

The college-student elves had long since

fled, but Olivia and Ginger remained, both of them fascinated.

"She's crazy about him," Ginger said.

"Look, Ash," McCall went on smoothly, "I know we had that little misunderstanding over the cocktail waitress, but don't you think we ought to let bygones be bygones?"

This man worked for Tanner? Olivia thought, trying to catch up with the conversation. He didn't look like the type to work for anyone but himself — or maybe the president.

Where had Ashley met him?

And what was the story with the cocktail waitress?

"I was young and stupid," Ashley spouted, putting her hands on her hips.

"But very beautiful." Jack McCall sighed. "And you still are, Ash. It's good to see you again."

"I bet you said the same thing to the cocktail waitress!" Ashley cried.

Jack looked, Olivia thought, like a young, modern version of Cary Grant. Impishly chagrined and way too handsome. And where had she heard his name before?

"She meant nothing to me," Jack said.

Olivia rolled her eyes. What a charmer he was. But he and Ashley looked perfect together, even if Ashley *was* trembling with fury.

It was time to step in, before things escalated.

Olivia hurried over and took her sister by the arm, tugging her toward the kitchen and, at the same time, chiming rapid-fire at McCall, over one shoulder, "Hi. I'm Olivia O'Ballivan, Ashley's sister. Glad to meet you. Make yourself at home while I talk her into building an ice castle out of sugar, will you? Thanks."

"An *ice castle?*" Ashley demanded once they were in the kitchen.

"With turrets, and lights inside. I'll pay you big bucks. Who *is* that guy, Ash?"

Ashley's shoulders sagged. She blew out a breath, and her bangs fluttered in midair. "He's nobody," she said.

"Get real. I know passion when I see it."

"I knew him in college," Ashley admitted.

"You never mentioned dating the reincarnation of Cary Grant."

"He dropped me for a cocktail waitress. Why would I want to mention that? I felt like an idiot."

"That was a while ago, Ash."

"Don't you have to get back to work or something?"

Ginger meandered in. *"There'll be a hot*

259

time in the old town tonight," she said.

"Hush," Olivia said.

"I will *not* hush," Ashley said. "And what's this about a sugar ice castle with lights inside?"

"I need something special to give the Quinns for Christmas, and you're the only one I know with that kind of —"

"Time on her hands?" Ashley finished ominously.

"Talent," Olivia said sweetly. "The only one with that kind of *talent.*"

"You are *so* full of it."

Olivia batted her eyelashes. "But I'm your big sister, and you love me. I'm always there for you, and if you ever had a pet, I'd give it free veterinary care. For life."

"No sugar castle," Ashley said. "I have a million things to do, with all these guests checking in." She paused. "If I murdered Jack McCall, would you testify that I was with you and give me an alibi?"

"Only if you made me a few batches of your stupendous Christmas cookies so I could give them to Sophie and Tanner."

Ashley smiled in spite of her earlier ire, but pain lingered in her eyes, old and deep. Jack McCall *had* hurt her, and suddenly he seemed a whole lot less charming than before. "I'll bake the cookies," she said.

"God knows where I'll find the time, but I'll do it."

Olivia kissed her sister's cheek. "I'm beyond grateful. Are you really going to refuse to rent McCall a room?"

"It's Christmas," Ashley said musingly. "And anyway, if he's here, under my roof, I can find lots of ways to get back at him. By New Year's, he'll be *begging* to break the lease."

Olivia laughed, held up the armload of clothes. "Thanks, Ash," she said. "In this getup, I'll be a regular Cinderella."

"Shall I stay here and spy, or go back to the clinic with you?" Ginger inquired, looking from Ashley to Olivia.

"You're going with me," Olivia said on the way back to the living room. She'd have gone out the back way, as the fleeing elves probably had, but she wanted one more look at Jack McCall.

"I'm not going anywhere," Ashley argued, following. "I've still got to tie at least a hundred bows on the branches of the Christmas tree."

"I was talking to Ginger," Olivia explained breezily.

"And I suppose she talked back?" Ashley asked.

"Skeptic," Olivia said.

Jack McCall had taken off his coat, and his bag sat at the base of the stairs. Evidently he was planning to stay on. The poor guy probably had no idea how many passive-aggressive ways there were for a crafty bed-and-breakfast owner to make an unwanted guest hit the road.

Too much starch in the sheets.

Too much salt in the stew.

The possibilities were endless.

Olivia was smiling broadly as she and Ginger descended Ashley's front steps, headed for the Suburban.

Fat flakes of snow drifted down from a heavy sky as the entire population of Stone Creek and half of Indian Rock gathered in the town's tiny park for the annual tree-lighting ceremony.

Sophie stood at Olivia's left side, Tanner at her right.

Brad had been roped into being the MC, but it was an informal gig, and he didn't have to sing. He announced that the high school gym was all decked out for the carnival and the dance afterward, and reminded the crowd that all the proceeds would go to worthy causes.

An enormous live spruce awaited splendor, its branches dark and fragrant, strings of extension cord running from beneath it. Roots enclosed in burlap, it would be planted when the ground thawed, like all the other Stone Creek Christmas trees before it.

"Are we ready?" Brad asked, holding the switch.

"YES!" roared the townspeople in one happy voice.

Brad flipped the plastic lever, and what seemed like millions of tiny colored lights shimmered in the cold winter night, like stars trapped in the branches.

The applause sounded like a herd of cattle stampeding.

The din had barely subsided when sleigh bells jingled, right on cue.

Tanner grinned down at Olivia and took her hand. She felt a little trill, though she was a bit nervous because she'd already had to surreptitiously roll up her borrowed palazzo pants a couple of times.

"Could it be?" Brad said into the mic. "Could *Santa Claus* be right here in Stone Creek?"

The smaller children in the crowd waited in breathless silence, their eyes huge with wonder and anticipation.

It happened every year. Santa arrived on a tractor from the heavy-equipment rental place, bells jingling an accompaniment through a scratchy PA system, the man in the red suit waving and tossing candy and shouting, "Ho! Ho! *Ho!*"

This year was a little different, it turned out.

Kris Kringle himself drove the fancy tree-lot sleigh, the one with the brass runners, into the center of the park — pulled by seven real live reindeer and a donkey. He wore hands down the best Santa suit Olivia had ever seen, and instead of candy, he had a huge, bulky green velvet bag in the back of the sleigh.

"Very authentic," Tanner told Olivia, his eyes sparkling.

There were actual wrapped presents in the bag, they soon saw, and Kris Kringle distributed them, making sure every child received one.

Even Sophie, too old at twelve to believe in Santa, got a small red-and-white striped package.

Brad must have been behind the gifts, Olivia thought. Times were hard, and a lot of Stone Creek families had been out of work since late summer. It would be just like her brother to see that they got something for Christmas in a pride-sparing way like this.

"Wow," Sophie said, staring at the package, then casting a sidelong glance at Tanner. "Can I open it?"

"Why not?" Tanner asked, looking mystified. Olivia knew he was throwing a turkey-and-trimmings feast for the whole community on Christmas Day, down at the senior citizens' center — Sophie had spilled the beans about that — but he didn't seem to be in on the presents-for-every-kid-in-town thing.

Sophie ripped into the package, drew in a breath when she saw what it was — an exquisite miniature snow globe with horses inside, one like Shiloh, the other the spitting image of Butterpie.

"Is this from you, Dad?" she asked after swallowing hard.

Tanner was staring curiously at Kris Kringle, who glanced his way and smiled before turning his attention back to the children clamoring to pet the lone donkey and the seven reindeer.

"Gently, now," Kringle called, a right jolly old elf. "They have a long trip to make on Christmas Eve and they're not used to crowds."

"Can they fly?" one child asked. Olivia spotted the questioner, a little boy in outgrown clothes, clutching an unopened package in both hands. She'd gone to high school with his parents, both of whom had been drawing unemployment since the sawmill closed down for the winter. It was rumored that the husband had just been hired as a laborer at Tanner's construction site, but of course that didn't mean their Christmas would be plush. The family would have bills to catch up on.

"Why, of course they can fly, Billy Johnson," Kringle replied jovially.

"Oh, brother," Tanner sighed.

Mr. Kringle had gotten to know everybody in town, Olivia thought, just since the day after Thanksgiving. Otherwise he wouldn't have known Billy's name.

"What about the donkey?" a little girl inquired. Like Billy's, her clothes showed some wear, and she had a package, too, also unopened. Olivia didn't recognize her, figuring she and her family must be new in town. "There wasn't any *donkey* in the St. Nicholas story."

"I've had to improvise, Sandra," Kringle explained kindly. "One of my reindeer —" here he paused, sought and unerringly found Olivia's face in the gathering, and winked "— has been on vacation."

"Oh," said the little girl.

Brad, having left the stage after lighting

up the tree, had made his way through the crowd, carrying a snow suited, gurgling Mac on one hip. Like every other kid, Mac had a present, and he was bonking Brad on the head with it as they approached.

"The packages were a nice touch," Olivia said, drawing her brother aside.

"I was expecting Fred Stevens, stuffed into the chamber of commerce's ratty old corduroy suit and driving a tractor," Brad said, looking puzzled. Even when *they* were kids, Mr. Stevens, a retired high school principal and the grand poo-bah at the lodge, had done the honors. "And I don't know anything about the presents."

No one else in Stone Creek, besides Tanner, had the financial resources to buy and wrap so many gifts. Olivia narrowed her eyes. "You can level with me," she whispered. "I know you and Meg arranged for this, just like when you made a lot of toys and food baskets magically appear on certain people's porches last Christmas Eve. You put one over on poor Fred somehow and paid Kringle to fill in."

Brad frowned. Took the present from Mac's hand, putting an end to the conking. "No, I didn't," he said. "Fred loves this job. I wouldn't have talked him out of it."

"Okay, but you must have bought the

presents. I *know* the town council, the chamber of commerce, both churches *and* the lodge couldn't have pulled this off."

"I haven't got a clue where these packages came from," Brad insisted, and his gaze strayed to Kris Kringle, who was preparing to drive away in his sleigh. "Unless . . ."

"Don't be silly," Olivia said. "The man runs a Christmas-tree lot and makes personal appearances at birthday parties. Wyatt ran a background check on him, and there's no way he could afford a giveaway on this scale. Nor, my dear brother, is he Santa Claus."

Brad shoved a hand through his hair, scanning the crowd, probably looking for his wife. "Look, I admit Meg and I are planning to scatter a few presents around town this year," he told her earnestly. "But if I was in on this one, believe me, I'd tell you."

Sophie stood nearby, shaking her snow globe for Mac's benefit. The baby strained over Brad's shoulder, trying to grab it.

Olivia turned to Tanner. "Then you must have done it."

"I wish I had," Tanner said thoughtfully. "The turkey dinner on Christmas Day seemed more practical to me." He grinned, putting one arm around Sophie and one around Olivia. "Let's go check out that carnival."

A look passed between Brad and Tanner.

"Have fun," Brad said, with a note of irony and perhaps warning in his voice.

"We will," Tanner replied lightly, slugging Brad in the Mac-free arm.

Brad gave him an answering slug.

Men, Olivia thought.

The carnival, like the tree-lighting ceremony, was crowded. The gym had been decorated with red and green streamers and giant gold Christmas balls, and there were booths set up on all four walls — fudge for sale in this one, baked goods in that one. Adults settled in for a rousing evening of bingo, the prizes all donated by local merchants, and there were games for the children — the "fishing hole" being the most popular.

For a modest fee, a child could dangle a long wooden stick with a string on the end of it over a shaky blue crepe-paper wall. After a tug, they'd pull in their line and find an inexpensive toy attached.

Sophie was soon bored, though good-naturedly so. She kept taking the snow globe out of her purse and shaking it to watch the snow swirl around Shiloh and Butterpie.

Tanner bought her a chili dog and a Coke and asked if she was ready to go home. She said she was.

"Ride along?" Tanner asked Olivia.

"I think I'll sit in on a round of bingo," she answered. The ladies from her church were running the game, and they'd been beckoning her to join in from the beginning.

Tanner nodded. "Save the first dance for me," he whispered into her ear. "And the last. And all the ones in between."

Feeling like a teenager at her first prom, Olivia nodded.

"It's weird that that guy knows about Butterpie and Shiloh," Sophie commented, munching on the chili dog as she and Tanner headed for Starcross in the truck. The snow was coming down so thick and fast that Tanner had the windshield wipers on. "A *nice* kind of weird, though."

"It must have been a coincidence, Soph."

"Heaven forbid," Sophie said loftily, "that I might want to believe in one teeny, tiny Christmas *miracle.*"

He thought of the dreams. Sophie as a lonely adult, working too hard, with no life outside her medical practice. A chill rippled down his spine, even though the truck's heater was going full blast. "Believe, Sophie," he said quietly. "Go ahead and believe."

He felt her glance, quick and curious. "What?"

"Maybe I *have* been too serious about things."

"Ya think?" Sophie quipped, but there was a taut thread of hope strung through her words, and it sliced deep into Tanner's heart.

"Look, I've been thinking — how would you like to go to school in Phoenix? There's a good one there, with an equestrian program and excellent security. I was going to wait until Christmas to bring it up, but —"

"I'd rather go to Stone Creek Middle School."

What had he expected her to say? The place was still a boarding school, even if it did have horse facilities. "I know that, Sophie. But I travel a lot and —"

"And Aunt Tessa will be here, so I'd be fine if you were away." Sophie was watching him closely. "What are you so afraid of, Dad?"

He thrust out a sigh. "That you'll be hurt. Your mom —"

"Dad, this is Stone Creek. There aren't any terrorists here. There's nobody to be mad and want to shoot at us because you built some bridge for the U.S. government where the local bomb-brewers didn't *want* a bridge."

Tanner's hands tightened on the steering wheel. He'd had no idea Sophie knew that much. Did she know about the periodic death threats, too? The ones that had prompted him to hire Jack McCall's men-in-black to guard Briarwood? Hell, he'd even had a detail looking out for Sophie when she was on the horse farm every summer, with Tessa.

"I feel safe here, Dad," Sophie went on gently. "I want you to feel safe, too. But you don't, because Uncle Jack wouldn't be in town if you did."

"How did you know Jack was here? He didn't get in until today."

"I saw him at the carnival with a pretty blond lady who didn't seem to like him," Sophie answered matter-of-factly. "Some kids play 'Where's Waldo?' Thanks to you, *I* play 'Where's Jack?' And I'm *real* good at spotting him."

"He's here on personal business," Tanner said. "Not to trail you."

"What kind of personal business?"

"How would I know? Jack doesn't tell me everything — he's got a private side." A "private side"? The man rappelled down walls of compounds behind enemy lines. He rescued kidnap victims and God knew what else. Tanner didn't have a lot of information about Jack's operation, beyond services rendered on Sophie's behalf at very high fees, and he didn't want to.

He slept better that way, and Jack, the secretive bastard, wouldn't have told him anyhow.

Oh, yeah. He was *way* happier. Except when he dreamed about Dr. Sophie Quinn, ghost of Christmas future, or thought about leaving Stone Creek and probably never seeing Olivia again.

"Soph," he said, skidding a little on the turnoff to Starcross, "when you grow up, are you going to hate me for making you go to boarding school?"

"I could never hate you, Dad." She said the words with such gentle equanimity that Tanner's throat constricted. "I know you're doing the best you can."

Sigh.

"I thought you'd be happy about Phoenix," he said after a pause. "It's only two hours from here, you know."

"What will that matter, if you're in some country where they want to put your head on a pike because you build things?"

It was a good thing they'd reached the driveway at Starcross; if they'd still been on the highway, Tanner might have run the truck into the ditch. "Is that what you think is going to happen?"

"I worry about it all the time. I'm human, you know."

"You're way too smart to be human. You're an alien from the Planet Practical."

She laughed, but there wasn't much humor in the sound. "I watch CNN all the time when you're out of the country," she confessed. "Sometimes really bad things happen to contractors working overseas."

Tanner pulled the truck up close to the house. He was anxious to get back to Olivia, but not so anxious that he'd leave Sophie in the middle of a conversation like this one. "What if I promised not to work outside the U.S.A., Soph? Ever again?"

The look of reluctant hope on the face Sophie turned to Tanner nearly broke him down. "You'd do that?"

"I'd do that, shorty."

She flung herself across the console, after springing the seat belt, and threw both arms around his neck, hugging him hard. He felt her tears against his cheek, where their faces touched. "Can I tell Aunt Tessa?" she sniffled.

"Yes," he said gruffly, holding on to her. Wishing she'd always be twelve, safe with him and Tessa at Starcross Ranch, and never become a relationship-challenged adult working eighteen-hour days out of loneliness as much as ambition.

It would be his fault if Sophie's life turned out that way. He'd been the one to set the bad example.

"I love you, Soph," he said.

She gave him a smacking kiss on the cheek and pulled away. "Love you, too, Dad," she replied, turning to get out of the truck.

He walked her inside the house, torn between wanting to stay home and wanting to be with Olivia.

Tessa had the tree lights on, and she and the puppies were cozied up together on the couch, watching a Christmas movie on TV.

"Dad is never going to work outside the country again!" Sophie shouted gleefully, bounding into the room like a storm trooper.

"Is that so?" Tessa asked, smiling, her gaze pensive as she studied Tanner. Was that skepticism he saw in her eyes?

"Dad's going back to dance the night away with Olivia," Sophie announced happily. "How about some hot chocolate, Aunt Tessa? I know how to make it."

"Good idea," Tessa said.

Sophie said a quick goodbye to Tanner as she passed him on her way to the kitchen.

"I hope you're going to keep your word," Tessa told him when Sophie was safely out of earshot.

"Why wouldn't I?"

"It's tempting, all that money. All those adrenaline rushes."

"I can resist temptation."

Tessa grinned. "Except where Olivia O'Ballivan is concerned, I suspect. Go ahead and 'dance the night away.' I'll take good care of Sophie, and if the place is over-run by revenge-seeking foreign extremists, I'll be sure and give you a call."

Tanner chuckled. Something inside him let go suddenly, something that had held on for dear life ever since that awful day on a street thousands of miles away, when Kat had died in his arms. "I *have* been a little paranoid, haven't I?" he asked.

"A little?" Tessa teased.

"There's a lady waiting at the bingo table," he told his sister. "Gotta go."

"See you tomorrow," Tessa said knowingly.

He let that one pass, waggling his fingers in farewell.

"Later, Soph!" he called.

And then he left the house, sprinting for

his truck.

"I need to get out of these pants before I kill myself," Olivia confided several hours later, when they'd both worn out the soles of their shoes dancing to the lodge orchestra's Christmas retrospective.

Tanner laughed. "Far be it from me to interfere," he said. Then he tilted his head back and looked up. "Is that mistletoe?"

"No," Olivia said. "It's three plastic Christmas balls hanging from a ribbon."

"Have you no imagination? No vision?"

"I can imagine myself in something a lot more comfortable than my sister's clothes," she told him. "I really hate to face it, but I'm going to have to *shop*."

"A woman who hates shopping," Tanner commented. "Will you marry me, Olivia O'Ballivan?"

It was a joke, and Olivia knew that as well as he did, but an odd, shivery little silence fell between them just the same. She seemed to draw away from him a little, even though he was holding her close as they swayed to the music.

"Let's get out of here," he said. Not exactly a mood enhancer, he reflected ruefully, but it was an honest sentiment.

She nodded. The pulse was beating at the

base of her throat again.

The snow hadn't let up — it was worse, if anything — and Tanner drove slowly back over the same course he'd followed with Sophie earlier that evening.

"Seriously," he began, picking up the conversation they'd had on the dance floor as though there had been no interval between then and now, "do you plan on getting married? Someday, I mean? Having kids and everything?"

Olivia gnawed on her lower lip for a long moment. "Someday, maybe," she said at last.

"What kind of guy would you be looking for?"

She smiled, until she saw that he was serious. The realization, like the pulse, was visible. "Well, he'd have to love animals, and be okay with my getting called out on veterinary emergencies at all hours of the day and night. It would be nice if he could cook, since I'm in the remedial culinary group." She paused, watching him. "And the sex would have to be very, very good."

He laughed again. "Is there an audition?"

"As a matter of fact, there is," she said. "Tonight."

Heat rushed through Tanner. If she kept talking like that, the windshield would fog up, making visibility even worse.

When they arrived at Olivia's place Ginger greeted them at the door, wanting to go outside.

He'd have to love animals . . .

Tanner took Ginger out and waited in the freezing cold until she'd done what she had to do.

Olivia was waiting when he got back inside. "Hungry?" she asked.

It would be nice if he could cook. . . .

Was she testing him?

"I could whip up an omelet," he offered.

She crossed to him, put her arms around his neck. "Later," she said.

And the sex would have to be very, very good.

Five minutes later, after some heavy kissing, he was helping her out of the palazzo pants. And everything *else* she was wearing.

CHAPTER TWELVE

He'd gone and fallen in love, Tanner realized, staring up at the ceiling as the first light of dawn crept across it. Olivia, sleeping in the curve of his arm, naked and soft, snuggled closer.

He loved her.

When had it happened? The first time they met, in his barn? Thanksgiving afternoon, before, during or after the kind of sex he'd never expected to have again? Or last night, at the dance?

Did it matter?

It was irrevocable. A no-going-back kind of thing.

He stirred to look at the clock on the bedside stand. Almost eight — Sophie would be up and on her way to school on the bus, well aware that dear old Dad hadn't come home last night.

What had Tessa told her?

He spoke Olivia's name.

She sighed and cuddled up closer.

"Doc," he said, more forcefully. "It's morning."

She bolted upright, looked at the clock. Shot out of bed. Realizing she was naked, she pulled on a pink robe. Her cheeks were the same color. "What are you doing here?" she demanded.

"You *know* what I'm doing here," he pointed out, in no hurry to get out of the warm bed.

"That was last night," she said, shoving a hand through her hair.

"Was I supposed to sneak out before sunrise? If I was, you didn't mention it."

Her color heightened. "What will Sophie think?"

"She's probably praying we'll get married, so she'll have a mom. She wants to grow up in Stone Creek."

To his surprise, Olivia's eyes filled with tears.

"Hey," he said, flinging back the covers and going to her, and the cold be damned. "What's the matter, Doc?" he asked, taking her into his arms.

"I love you," she sobbed into his bare shoulder. "That's what's wrong!"

He held her away, just far enough to look into her upturned face. "No, Doc," he

281

murmured. "That's what's *right.*"

"What?"

"I love you, too," he said. "And it's cold out here. Can I share that bathrobe?"

She laughed and tried to stretch the sides of it around him. Her face felt wet against his chest. "This all happened so fast," she said. Then she tilted her head back and looked up at him again. "Are you sure? It wasn't just — just the sex?"

"The sex was world-class," he replied, kissing the top of her head. "But it's a lot more than that. The way you tried to cheer Butterpie up. That goofy reindeer you rescued, and the fact that you ran a background check on his owner. The old Suburban, and your grandfather's jacket, and that pitiful-looking little Christmas tree."

"What happens now?"

"We have sex again?"

She punched him, but she was grinning, all wet faced and happy. And his butt was freezing, since the robe didn't cover it. "Not that. Tomorrow. Next week. Next month . . ."

"We date. We sleep together, whenever we get the chance." He caught his hand under her chin and gently lifted. "We rename the ranch and renovate the house."

"Rename the ranch?"

"You said it once. 'Starcross' isn't a happy name. What do you want to call it, Doc?"

She wriggled against him. "How about 'Star*fire* Ranch'?" she asked.

"Works for me," he said, about to kiss her. Steer her back to bed. Hell, they were both late — might as well make it count.

"Wait," she said, pulling back. Her eyes were huge and blue and if he fell into them, he'd drown. And count himself lucky for it. "What about Sophie? Does she get to stay in Stone Creek?"

"She stays," Tanner said, after heaving a sigh.

"We'll keep her safe, Tanner," Olivia said. "Together."

He nodded.

And they went back to bed, though the lovemaking came a long time later.

Tanner told Olivia all about Kat, and how she'd died, and how he'd blamed himself and feared for Sophie.

And Olivia told him about her mother, and how she'd left the family. How her father had died, and her grandfather had carried on after that as best he could. How it was when animals talked to her.

When the deepest, most private things had been said, and only then, they made love.

■ ■ ■ ■

On the morning of Christmas Eve, Olivia stood in a hospital corridor, peering through a little window at the main reason she'd been afraid to get married, long before she met Tanner Quinn.

He waited downstairs, in the lobby. She had to do this alone, but it was better than nice to know he was there.

Olivia closed her eyes for a moment, rested her forehead against the glass.

Restless, unhappy, Delia had left a husband and four children behind one blue-skyed summer day. Just gotten on a bus and boogied.

Olivia's worst fear, one she'd successfully sublimated for as long as she could remember, was that the same heartless streak might be buried somewhere in *her,* as well. That it might surface suddenly, causing her to abandon people and animals who loved and trusted her.

It was a crazy idea — she knew that. She was the steady type, brave, thrifty, loyal and true.

But then, Delia had seemed that way, too. She'd read Ashley and Melissa bedtime stories and listened to their prayers, played hide-and-seek with them while she was hanging freshly laundered sheets in the backyard, let Olivia wear clear nail polish even over her dad's protests. She'd taken all four of them to afternoon movies, sometimes even on school days, where they shared a big bucket of popcorn. She'd helped Brad with his homework practically every night.

And then she'd left.

Without a word of warning she'd simply vanished.

Why?

Olivia opened her eyes.

The woman visible through that window didn't look as though she could answer that question or any other. She'd retreated inside herself, according to her doctors, and she might not come out again.

It happened with people who had abused alcohol and drugs over a long period of time, the doctors had said.

Olivia drew a deep breath, pushed open the door and went in.

Everyone had a dragon to fight. This was hers.

Delia looked too small to have caused so much trouble and heartache, and too broken. Huddled in a chair next to a tabletop Christmas tree decorated with paper chains and nothing else, she looked at Olivia with mild interest, then looked away again.

Olivia crossed to her, touched her thin shoulder.

She flinched away. Though she didn't speak, the look in her eyes said, *Leave me alone.*

"It's me, Mom," she said. "Olivia."

Delia simply stared, giving no sign of recognition.

Olivia dropped to a crouch beside her mother's chair. "I guess I'll never know why you left us," she said moderately, "and maybe it doesn't matter now. We turned out well, all of us."

Delia's vacant eyes were a soft, faded blue, like worn denim, or a fragile spring sky. Slowly, almost imperceptibly, she nodded.

Tears burned Olivia's eyes. "I'm in love, Mom," she said. "His name is Tanner. Tanner Quinn, and he has a twelve-year-old daughter, Sophie. I — I want to be a good stepmother to Sophie, and I guess, in some strange way, I needed to see you to know I could do this. That I could really be a wife and a mother —"

Delia didn't speak. She didn't cry or embrace her daughter or ask for a second chance. In short, there was no miracle.

And yet Olivia felt strangely light inside,

as though there had been.

"Anyway, I'm planning to come back and see you as often as I can." She stood up straight again, opened her purse. Took out a small wrapped package. It was a bulb in a prepared planter, guaranteed to bloom even in the dead of winter. She'd wanted to bring perfume — one of her memories of Delia was that she'd loved smelling good — but that was on the hospital's forbidden gift list, because of the alcohol content. "Merry Christmas, Mom."

I'm not you.

She laid the parcel in Delia's lap, bent to kiss the top of her head and left.

Downstairs, Tanner drew her into a hug. Kissed her temple. "You gonna be okay, Doc?" he asked.

"Better than okay," she answered, smiling up at him. "Oh, much, much better than okay."

At six o'clock straight up, Kris Kringle officially closed the tree lot. He'd sold every one — nothing left now but needles and twine. The plastic reindeer and the hired Santa were gone, but the sleigh was still there.

He looked up and down the street.

Folks were inside their warm lighted

houses and their churches now, as they should be on Christmas Eve. When he was sure nobody was looking, he gave a soft whistle.

The reindeer came — all except Rodney, that is. Took their usual places in front of the sleigh, waiting to be hitched up.

He frowned. Where was that deer?

The clippity-clop of small hooves sounded behind him on the pavement. He turned, and there was Rodney, coming toward him out of that snowy darkness, ready to take his first flight. The donkey had filled in willingly at the tree-lighting, but this was the real deal — and everybody knew donkeys couldn't fly.

"Ready?" he asked, bending over Rodney and stroking his silvery back.

He fitted the harnesses gently, having had years of practice. Climbed into the sleigh and took up the reins. They'd have to stop off at home, so he could change into his traveling clothes and, of course, fetch the first bag of gifts.

First stop, he decided: Olivia O'Ballivan's house. She'd been so kind to that little tree — next year at this time, he knew, it would be growing tall and strong on the grounds of the new shelter, glowing with colored lights.

Yes, sir. He'd deliver her present first. That woman needed a new coffeepot.

Christmas Eve, the weather was crisp and clear with the promise of snow, and Olivia felt renewed as she watched Tanner's respectably muddy extended-cab truck coming up the driveway. They were all invited to Stone Creek Ranch for the evening — she and Tanner, Tessa and Sophie — and she knew it would be like old times, when Big John was alive. He'd always roped in half the countryside to share in the celebration.

Her heart soared a little when she heard Tanner's footsteps on the back porch, followed by his knock.

She opened the door, looked up at him with shining eyes.

He took in her red velvet skirt and matching crepe sweater with an appreciative grin, looking pretty darn handsome himself in jeans, a white shirt and his black leather jacket.

"Olivia O'Ballivan," he said with a twinkling grin. "You *shopped.*"

"I sure did," she replied happily. "That big box of presents you passed on the porch is further proof. How about loading it up for me, cowboy?"

Tanner bent to greet Ginger, who could barely contain her glee at his arrival. "Anything for you, ma'am," Tanner drawled, still admiring Olivia's Christmas getup. "Tessa and Sophie went on ahead in Tessa's rig," he added, to explain their absence. "I told them we'd be right behind them."

He straightened, and Ginger went back to her bed.

"She's not going with us?" Tanner asked, referring, of course, to the dog.

"She claims she's expecting a visitor," Olivia said.

Tanner's grin quirked one corner of his kissable mouth. "Well, then," he said, making no move to leave the kitchen *or* load up the box of presents.

"What?" Olivia asked, shrugging into her good coat.

"I have something for you," Tanner said, and for all his worldliness, he looked and sounded shy. "But I'm wondering if it's too soon."

Olivia's heartbeat quickened. She waited, watching him, hardly daring to breathe.

It couldn't be. They'd only just agreed that they loved each other. . . .

Finally Tanner gave a decisive, almost rueful sigh, crossed to her, laid his hands on her shoulders and gently pressed her into one of the chairs at the kitchen table. Then, just like in an old movie, or a romantic story, he dropped to one knee.

"Will you marry me, Olivia O'Ballivan?" he asked. "When you're darn good and ready and the time is right?"

"Say yes," Ginger said from the dog bed.

As if Olivia needed any canine input. "Yes," she said with soft certainty. "When we're *both* darn good and ready, and we *agree* that the time is right."

Eyes shining with love, and what looked like relief — had he really thought she might refuse? — Tanner reached into his jacket pocket and brought out a small white velvet box. An engagement ring glittered inside, as dazzling as a captured star.

"I love you," Tanner said. "But if you don't want to wear this right away, I'll understand."

Because she couldn't speak, Olivia simply extended her left hand. Tears of joy blurred her vision, making the diamond in her engagement ring seem even bigger and brighter than it was.

Tanner slid it gently onto her finger, and it fit perfectly, gleaming there.

Olivia laughed, sniffled. "To think I got you a bathrobe!" she blubbered.

Tanner laughed, too, and stood, pulling

Olivia to her feet, drawing her into his arms and sealing the bargain with a long, slow kiss.

"We'd better get going," he said with throaty reluctance when it was over.

Olivia nodded.

Tanner went to lug the box of gifts to the truck, while Olivia lingered to unplug Charlie Brown's bubbling lights.

"You're sure you won't come along?" she asked Ginger, pausing in the kitchen.

"I'll just settle my brains for a long winter's nap," Ginger said, muzzle on forepaws, gazing up at Olivia with luminous brown eyes. *"Don't be surprised if Rodney's gone when you get to the ranch. It's Christmas Eve, and he has work to do."*

"I'll miss him," Olivia said, reaching for her purse.

But Ginger was already asleep, perhaps with visions of rawhide sugarplums dancing in her head.

Stone Creek Ranch was lit up when Olivia and Tanner arrived, and the yard was crowded with cars and trucks.

"There's something I need to do in the barn," Olivia told Tanner as he wedged the rig into one of the few available parking spaces. "Meet you inside?"

He smiled, leaned across the console and

kissed her lightly. "Meet you inside," he said.

Rodney's stall was empty, and Olivia felt a pang at that.

She stood there for a while, marveling at the mysteries of life in general and Christmas in particular, and was not surprised when Brad joined her.

"When I came out to feed the horses," he told Olivia, "there was no sign of Rodney the reindeer. I figured he got out somehow and wandered off, but there were no tracks in the snow. It's as if he vanished."

Olivia dried her eyes. "It's Christmas Eve," she said, repeating Ginger's words. "He has work to do." She turned, looked up at her brother. "He's all right, Brad. Trust me on that."

Brad chuckled and wrapped an arm around her shoulders. "If you say so, Doc, I believe you, but I'm going to miss the little guy, just the same."

"Me, too," Olivia said.

Brad took her hand, examined the ring. "That's quite the sparkler," he said gravely. "Are you sure about this, Liv?"

"Very sure," she said.

He kissed her forehead. "That's good enough for me," he told her.

Together they went into the house, where there was music and laughter and a tall tree, all alight. Olivia spotted Ashley and Melissa right away, and some of Meg's family, the McKettricks, were there, too.

Sophie rushed to greet Olivia. "I get to stay in Stone Creek!" she confided, her face aglow with happiness. "Dad said so!"

Olivia laughed and hugged the child. "That's wonderful news, Sophie," she said.

"I've been thinking I might want to be a veterinarian when I grow up, like you," Sophie said seriously.

"Plenty of time to decide," Olivia replied gently. Just as she'd fallen in love with Tanner, hard, fast and forever, she'd fallen in love with Sophie, too. She'd never try to replace Kat, of course, but she'd be the best possible stepmother.

"Dad told me he was going to ask you to marry him," Sophie added, her voice soft now as she took Olivia's hand and smiled to see her father's engagement ring shining on the appropriate finger. "He wanted to know if it was okay with me, and I said yes." A mischievous smile curved the girl's lips. "I see you did, too."

"I've never been a stepmother before, Sophie," Olivia said, her eyes burning again. "Will you be patient with me until I get the hang of it?"

"I'm almost a teenager," Sophie reminded

her sagely. "I suppose you'll have to be patient with me, too."

"I can manage," Olivia assured her.

Sophie's gaze strayed, came to rest on Tessa, who was off by herself, sipping punch and watching the hectic proceedings with some trepidation, like a swimmer working up the courage to jump into the water. "I'm a little worried about Aunt Tessa, though," the child admitted. "She's been hurt a lot worse than she's letting on."

"This crowd can be a little overwhelming," Olivia replied. "Let's help her get to know some of her new neighbors."

Sophie nodded, relieved and happy.

Arm in arm, she and Olivia went to join Tessa.

"You're coming to my open house tomorrow, right?" Ashley asked hopefully, sometime later, when they'd all had supper and opened piles of gifts, and the two sisters had managed a private moment over near the fireplace.

"Of course," Olivia said, pleased that Ashley looked and sounded like her old self. "Did you manage to get rid of Jack McCall yet?"

Ashley's blue eyes shone like sapphires. "The man is impossible to get rid of," she said, nodding toward the Christmas tree, where Jack stood talking quietly with Keegan McKettrick. As if sensing Ashley's gaze, he lifted his punch cup to her in a saucy toast and nodded. "But I'm having fun trying."

Olivia laughed. "Maybe you shouldn't try *too* hard," she said.

Soon after that, with little Mac nodding off, exhausted by all the excitement, people started leaving for their own homes.

Merry Christmases were exchanged all around.

Olivia left with Tanner, delighted to see a soft snow falling as they drove toward home.

"I meant to congratulate you on how dirty this truck is," Olivia teased.

"I finally found a mud puddle," Tanner admitted with a grin.

It felt good to laugh with him.

They parted reluctantly, on Olivia's back porch. She'd be going to Ashley's tomorrow, while Tanner spent Christmas Day with Tessa and Sophie, at *Starfire* Ranch.

He kissed her thoroughly and murmured a Merry Christmas, and finally took his leave.

Olivia went inside, found Ginger waiting just on the other side of the kitchen door.

"Did your visitor show up?" Olivia asked as Ginger went past her for a necessary pit stop in the back yard.

"See for yourself," Ginger said as she climbed the porch steps again, to go inside with Olivia.

Puzzled, Olivia looked around. Nothing seemed different — and yet something was. But what?

Ginger waited patiently, until Olivia finally noticed. A brand-new coffeemaker gleamed on the countertop, topped with a fluffy red bow.

Tanner couldn't have brought it, she thought, mystified. Perhaps Tessa and Sophie had dropped it off? But that wasn't possible, either — they'd already been at Stone Creek Ranch when Tanner and Olivia arrived.

"Ginger, who — ?"

Ginger didn't say anything at all. She just turned and padded into the living room.

Olivia followed, musing. Brad? Ashley or Melissa?

No. Brad and Meg had given her a dainty gold bracelet for Christmas, and the twins had gone together on a spa day at a fancy resort up in Flagstaff.

The living room was dark, and Christmas Eve was almost over, so Olivia decided to light the tree and sit quietly for a while with Ginger, reliving all the wonderful moments of the day, tucking them away, one by one, within the soft folds of her heart.

Tanner, proposing marriage on one knee, in her plain kitchen.

Sophie, thrilled that she'd be a permanent resident of Stone Creek from now on. She could ride Butterpie every day, and she was already boning up on Emily's lines in *Our Town,* determined to be ready for the auditions next fall.

Ashley, so recently broken, now happily bedeviling a certain handsome boarder.

Olivia cherished these moments, and many others besides.

She leaned over to plug in Charlie Brown's lights, and that was when she saw the card tucked in among the branches.

Her fingers trembled a little as she opened the envelope.

The card showed Santa and his reindeer flying high over snowy rooftops, and the handwriting inside was exquisitely old-fashioned and completely unfamiliar.

Happy Christmas, Olivia. Think of us on cold winter mornings, when you're enjoying your coffee. With appreciation for your kindness, Kris Kringle and Rodney.

"No way," Olivia marveled, turning to Ginger.

"*Way,*" Ginger said. "*I told you I was expecting company.*"

And just then, high overhead, sleigh bells jingled.

"You look mighty handsome in that apron, cowboy," Olivia said, joining Tanner, Tessa and Sophie behind the cafeteria counter at Stone Creek High School on Christmas Day. It was almost two o'clock — time for the community Christmas dinner — and there was a crowd waiting outside. "You're understaffed, though."

Tanner's blue-denim eyes lit at the sight of Olivia taking her place beside him and tying on an apron she'd brought from home. Tessa and Sophie exchanged pleased looks, but neither spoke.

A fancy catering outfit out of Flagstaff had decorated the tables and prepared the food — turkey and prime rib and ham, and every imaginable kind of trimming and salad and holiday dessert — and they'd be clearing tables and cleaning up afterward. But Olivia knew, via Sophie, that Tanner had insisted on doing more than paying the bill.

A side door opened, and Brad and Meg came in, followed by Ashley and Melissa, fresh from Ashley's open house at the bed-and-breakfast. They were all pushing up their sleeves as they approached, ready to lend a hand. Meg was especially cheerful, since Carly had shared in the festivities, via speakerphone. She'd be back in Stone Creek soon after New Year's, eager to take Sophie under her wing and "show her the ropes."

Of course, having spent the morning at Ashley's herself, Olivia had been expecting them.

Tanner swallowed, visibly moved. "I never thought — I mean, it's Christmas, and . . ."

Olivia gave him a light nudge with her elbow. "It's what country people do, Tanner," she told him. "They help. Especially if they're family."

"Shall I let them in before they break down the doors?" Brad called, grinning. He didn't seem to mind that he looked a little silly in the bright red sweater Ashley had knitted for his Christmas gift. On the front, she'd stitched in a cowboy Santa Claus, strumming a guitar.

Tanner nodded, after swallowing again. "Let them in," he said. Then he turned to Olivia, Tessa and Sophie. "Ready, troops?"

They had serving spoons in hand. Sophie even sported a chef's hat, strung with battery-operated lights.

"Ready!" chorused the three women who loved Tanner Quinn.

Brad opened the cafeteria doors and in they came, the ones who were down on their luck, or elderly, or simply lonely. The children were spruced up in their Sunday best, wide-eyed and shy. Some carried toys they'd received from Brad and Meg in last night's secret-Santa front-porch blitz, others wore new clothes and a few of the older ones were rocking to MP3 players.

Ashley, Melissa and Meg ushered the elderly ladies and gentlemen to tables, took their orders and brought them plates.

Everyone else went through the line — proud, hardworking men who might have been ashamed to partake of free food, even on a holiday, if the whole town hadn't been invited to join in, tired-looking women who'd had one too many disappointments but were daring to hope things could be better, teenagers doing their best to be cool.

As she filled plate after plate, Olivia felt her throat constrict with love for these townspeople — *her* people, the home folks — and for Tanner Quinn. After all, this dinner had been his idea, and he'd spent a fortune to make it happen.

She was most touched, though, when the

mayor showed up, and a dozen of the town's more prosperous families. They had fine dinners waiting at home, and Christmas trees surrounded by gifts — but they'd come to show that this was no charity event.

It was for everybody, and their presence made that plain.

When the last straggler had been served, when plates had been wrapped in foil for delivery to shut-ins, and the caterers had loaded the copious leftovers in their van for delivery to the nursing home, the people of Stone Creek lingered, swapping stories and jokes and greetings.

This, Olivia thought, watching them, seeing the new hope in their eyes, *is Christmas.*

Inevitably, Brad's guitar appeared.

He sat on the edge of one of the tables, tuned it carefully and cleared his throat.

A silence fell, fairly buzzing with anticipation.

"I'm not doing this alone," Brad said, grinning as he addressed the gathering. All these people were his friends and, by extension, his family. To Olivia, it was a measure of his manhood that he could wear that sweater in public. He knew how hard Ashley had worked to prepare her gift, and because he loved his kid sister, he didn't mind the amused whispers.

A few chuckles rose from the tables. It was partly because of his words, Olivia supposed, and partly because of the sweater.

He strummed a few notes, and then he began to sing.

"Silent night, holy night . . ."

And voice by voice, cautious and confident, old and young, warbling alto and clear tenor, the carol grew, until all of Stone Creek was singing.

Olivia looked up into Tanner's eyes, and something passed between them, something silent and fundamental and infinitely precious.

"Do I qualify?" he asked her when the song faded away.

"As what?"

"A real cowboy," Tanner said with a grin teetering at the corners of his mouth.

Olivia stood on tiptoe and kissed him lightly. "Yes," she told him happily. "You're the real deal, Tanner Quinn."

"Was it the muddy truck?" he teased.

She laughed. "No," she answered, laying a hand to his chest and spreading her fingers wide. "It's that big, wide-open-spaces heart of yours."

He looked up, frowned ruefully. "No mistletoe," he said.

Olivia slipped her arms around his neck,

right there in the cafeteria at Stone Creek High School, with half the town looking on. "Who needs mistletoe?"

ABOUT THE AUTHOR

The daughter of a town marshal, **Linda Lael Miller** grew up in rural Washington. The self-confessed barn goddess was inspired to pursue a career as an author after an elementary school teacher said the stories she was writing might be good enough to be published.

Linda broke into publishing in the early 1980s. She is now a *New York Times* bestselling author of more than sixty contemporary, romantic suspense and historical novels, including *McKettrick's Choice, The Man from Stone Creek* and *Deadly Gamble.* When not writing, Linda enjoys riding her horses and playing with her cats and dogs. Through her Linda Lael Miller Scholarships for Women, she provides grants to women who seek to improve their lot in life through education.

For more information about Linda, her

scholarships and her novels, visit www.linda
laelmiller.com.

We hope you have enjoyed this Large Print book. Other Thorndike, Wheeler, Kennebec, and Chivers Press Large Print books are available at your library or directly from the publishers.

For information about current and upcoming titles, please call or write, without obligation, to:

Publisher
Thorndike Press
295 Kennedy Memorial Drive
Waterville, ME 04901
Tel. (800) 223-1244

or visit our Web site at:

http://gale.cengage.com/thorndike

OR

Chivers Large Print
published by AudioGO Ltd
St James House, The Square
Lower Bristol Road
Bath BA2 3BH
England
Tel. +44(0) 800 136919
email: info@audiogo.co.uk
www.audiogo.co.uk

All our Large Print titles are designed for easy reading, and all our books are made to last.